A PERFECT SNOW

A Junior Library Guild Selection

A Pacific Northwest Booksellers Association Award Winner

**A Children's Book Council
Notable Social Studies Trade Book**

"The story will likely get readers thinking about the changes people undergo and their own motivations and beliefs. [Readers] will come away with the realization that actions inevitably bear consequences, sometimes unexpected ones."
—*School Library Journal*

"Readers are immediately drawn into this story about a hate crime. Through descriptive language, the author skillfully reveals the dangers of fearing those who are not like us."
—*Notable Social Studies Trade Books for Young People*

"Bravo to Martin for her revealing, sensitive, and lecture-free approach to an all-too-common problem troubling teens across the nation."
—*The Midwest Book Review*

Nora Martin

is the author of several young adult novels, including *Flight of the Fisherbird*, *The Stone Dancers*, and the acclaimed *Eagle's Shadow*, which was a Bank Street College Best Book of the Year and an ALA Best Trade Book for Social Studies. She is a school librarian in rural Montana.

A PERFECT SNOW

by Nora Martin

BLOOMSBURY

For my sons. Brothers. Friends.

Published by Bloomsbury, New York and London
Distributed to the trade by Holtzbrinck Publishers

Library of Congress Cataloging-in-Publication Data
Martin, Nora.
A perfect snow / Nora Martin.
p. cm.
Summary: Seventeen-year-old Ben must deal with a violent white-supremacy hate group in his small Montana town because his father and his friends are involved with it.
ISBN 1-58234-788-3 (hardcover)
ISBN 1-58234-925-8 (paperback)
[1. Right-wing extremists—Fiction. 2. White supremacy movements—Fiction. 3. Prejudices—Fiction. 4. Montana—Fiction.] I. Title.
PZ7.M364155 Pe 2002   [Fic]—dc21   2001052577

Printed in Great Britain
1 3 5 7 9 10 8 6 4 2

Bloomsbury USA Children's Books
175 Fifth Avenue
New York, New York 10010

All papers used by Bloomsbury Publishing are natural, recyclable products made from wood grown in well-managed forests. The manufacturing processes conform to the environmental regulations of the country of origin.

·CHAPTER ONE·

SKY

In cold night emptiness, the metal and plastic of the car burned fast like a dry field. The heat blew over me until I glowed and grew with it. I thought the fumes in the gas tank might make the car explode. Around the burning metal mound the snow melted, making a black lake that reflected the fire skyward.

I pretended the car did not just belong to some Jew lawyer like the sign on the wall said—Cohen, Goldberg and Brown—but belonged to all the people I hated in this town. The smoke became them, drifting out of my life forever. I felt strong for the first time in months. With that one little match I had taken control.

Everything really started the day my younger brother, David, got jumped in the hall by that rich pig Jason Johnson. He was a guy who owned so many clothes, he just threw them away when they got dirty. The guy smelled like new cotton and he liked putting it in people's faces.

I was coming down the hall when I saw Johnson slug David, calling him a dumb redneck. My brother groaned as the air whooshed out of him and he slumped back against the lockers. I saw his face go pale. David's big, but he's actually a wimp when it comes to fighting. The strange thing is, I know he asks for it. He's the kind of wormy guy who calls other kids names under his breath and does annoying little things that make people mad. He does it to me too. It's like an addiction with him; he can't stop himself even when he ends up getting the crap beat out of him. But still, he's my brother.

When he noticed me I saw him mouth my name, "Ben," in a silent plea for help. I was on that rich guy before he could suck breath. I was glad to see blood running out of his nose, messing up that fancy shirt.

Almost as soon as I swung, the principal, Hard-Ass Harrison, hauled us to the office. Johnson, David and I got a day of in-school suspension. Of course the rich kid said David and I started it. I kept quiet; who would believe me, anyway? I'd heard that Johnson's dad paid for the school's new track, which explains a lot. Those rich guys can get away with about anything.

Driving home, I couldn't settle down until we got to the place I liked best: the spot right after the dip when the road curves up again. Here it looks as if the world comes to an end at the top of the hill, with nothing on the other side.

I accelerated hard, letting frustration push my foot: fifty, sixty miles an hour. The speed soaked into me. I hoped, as I always did, that the truck would keep going, up and up, even after the pavement dropped back to earth. Somewhere inside I believed the truck could soar above the snow-frozen fields toward the distant Tobacco Root Mountains. Then this ugly town, the school and the kids who looked down on our family would stay below and all I would see, feel and smell would be sky.

But of course, when the truck came over the crest of the hill, the tires stayed firmly on the road. I noticed David gripping the edge of his notebook, looking shook up.

"Ben, you won't tell Dad, will you?" he asked.

"No way," I said. What could he do, anyway? He knew as well as I did that David asked for it. "And don't mention our detention with the RETCH either."

David actually smiled for a second. "What's a RETCH?"

"A RETCH," I told him, "is a kid who's rich enough to cheat. Like Jason Johnson, who doesn't get in trouble as long as his old man has the checkbook handy." I knew Jason had been given the same punishment as we had but I wouldn't have been surprised if David and I were the only ones to show up in the detention room the next day.

David went back to his sullen stare. Slowing the truck down to thirty-five for the icy corner, I reached out and tugged at the collar of his jacket. "Relax," I said.

"Sure," he said. "I just got my guts smashed at school and now I'm speeding to my death with a worn-out Chevy pickup for a coffin."

"Oh, come on, David, 'fess up. What did you do to Johnson? Did you knock his books on the floor, or call him dumb-ass?"

"I didn't do anything," David argued.

But he always said that. I slowed the truck some more. In the distance, beyond a row of cottonwood trees, the twenty metal rectangular boxes of the trailer park where we lived came into sight.

David was still gripping the notebook. "What is it with you, anyway? You drive this truck like it's a race to hell."

I glanced at him. "I'm sick of being some kind of crap pile that people like Jason Johnson go out of their way to step over, holding their noses while they do it. It's been that way ever since we came to this armpit town. Lonn and the guys at the shop are the only people who've been okay to us."

In late August, just a week after we came to Lodgette, Dad met Lonn down at the café. Then Lonn invited him and us to join his Wednesday night meeting.

"In the four months we've been here, none of those guys, especially not Chuck and Travis, has ever been interested in me," David returned.

A couple of years older than us, Chuck and Travis were like Lonn's apprentices or something. They had taken to me from the first time David and I went to the meeting with Dad. But I knew why they ignored David.

"Don't act so eager to please them," I said. "It's like you'd turn yourself purple if they said to."

David stared at me. "Look who's talking, Mr. Big Man. It's not like they let you in on everything."

"They will."

"Maybe, but nobody else in Lodgette ever said boo to you," David said.

"I don't see you hanging out with guys from the football team that you quit," I snapped back at him.

"I've made some friends," David said.

"Oh, right. The cow kids fresh from the manure factory, they're as tough as gophers. Stick their heads out of the ground just long enough for people like Johnson to get a shot at them."

"We're cow kids too," he said. "Remember the stares we got when we first came to school?   Besides, you may wear a football uniform, but it doesn't mean you're part of the team. I wasn't going to be a bench warmer like you."

I felt bad for giving him a hard time. And he was right. If we were still in Prairie Springs, he would have made the varsity team, not just the junior varsity team. And he would have played in every game. But here in Lodgette he didn't have a chance.

A mile down the hill I pulled into the parking space left between the litter of oil barrels and car parts.

Our trailer sat on concrete blocks. Rust stains ran down the sides, as if over the years the trailer had bled and no one cared enough to bandage it.

"I don't think the landlord is ever going to clean this up," David said as we cut our way through the gray snow to the trailer.

9

As we passed by old Mrs. Kenny's trailer, I saw she was hauling out a large plastic turkey to put on her flat roof. As she started for the ladder I ran over to her.

"Jeez, Ben, what are you doing?" David called to me.

Mrs. Kenny waved to me as I approached. "Hello, Ben."

"Time for Thanksgiving already?" I teased as I took the turkey and climbed the ladder. I put it next to the tires that kept the metal roof from flapping in the wind. I anchored the worn plastic statue and jumped down. "There you are, Mrs. Kenny."

"You're a good neighbor, Ben," she said.

As I stepped through the rim of ice around our door, I saw Dad sitting in the old recliner in front of the TV. His ragged cowboy boots were tossed on the rug by the chair.

Suspended in a cloud of heat, Mom stood in the kitchen making dinner. I went for the refrigerator and grabbed the orange juice. "What's cooking?" I asked her.

"Meatloaf. Why are you so late tonight, Ben?"

I shrugged. "Couldn't get the Chevy started again. We had to jump it. I think it needs a new battery." I watched to see Dad's reaction.

He turned around and looked at me. His face was easy. *Maybe things went good for him today,* I thought.

"You've been saying that for a month, Ben." There was a note of teasing in his voice. "I keep hoping you'll stop at Lonn's garage. Have him show you a thing or two. There's nothing he likes better than to have you young guys at the shop with him."

"I'll do it," David offered. Dad ignored him. David couldn't please Dad as easy as I could. For a long time I had figured that it was because I was older and learned to do things before David did, but finally I realized it was because of the same old thing that always got David into trouble. He could never just be David. He was either too eager to please or pissed off and sulking.

Picking the football up off the floor, I perched on the arm of the sofa and started passing the ball hand to hand. "How'd job hunting go today?"

"Not so much as a bite," Dad said. "This town has no use for an old cowhand like me. Investment brokers and art dealers are the only guys that can get a job now. The Jew boys running everything make sure of that."

"Something will come along," I said.

"You still think there's a Santa Claus or a tooth fairy, don't you?" David said.

I threw the football at him. "Get a handle on it, David." I didn't want him to ruin Dad's mood.

David caught the ball, but he lost his balance and slammed against the kitchen wall, making the whole trailer shake. He went on, "It's just like you were saying about school, Ben. If you're not one of these guys with money, you don't have a chance."

I knew David was exactly right but I just didn't think we should discourage Dad right at that moment. "When calving season starts, there'll be need for an extra hand," I insisted.

"I'll only work on a real ranch. I don't want to work with California college kids, or people that don't speak English. Those people are just playing at being ranch hands," Dad said. "Like I told the new owners at the Triple T."

The Triple T was the ranch where we'd spent five years, back when I was between eight and thirteen. It was the best. There was a nice house for us to live in, green hills all around and good hunting right on the place. But actually we'd been at four ranches that I could remember and several more when I was real little. In every place it didn't take too long for Dad to find something he thought was wrong. Then he started complaining. He'd keep at it until he got fed up and quit or the owners would ask him to leave. Finally, this last time he couldn't find another ranch to go to. So we ended up here.

"You'd have a better chance if you were a Mexi wetback," I joked. "Then they'd jump to hire you. Maybe you should fake being a wetback, Dad. Dye your hair black and shuffle into the job saying, '*Sí, señor,* twelve kids, give job.'" Dad and David finally laughed.

"I did meet up with Lonn down at the Kitchen Café this morning," Dad said. "He invited me to join him and another guy for coffee."

"What guy?" I asked.

"Someone new. He's never been to the meeting, but he just bought the Quick Mart up by the highway." Dad's eyes were starting to glitter as they did when he was excited about something. "Lonn said, right to the guy, that I needed a job."

"It's sure not like when you were boss on the ranches," I said. "Then it was you that passed out the jobs." As soon as I said it I was sorry. Dad's face scrunched up in angry lines. *Damn*, I swore to myself.

"Anyway," Dad said, "this new guy said he'd come to the meeting tonight. You boys make a good show for him."

"Sure thing," David said. "Let's play up to this guy. Maybe he can get work for all of us."

"You make this Lonn sound like some kind of superman," Mom said over the sound of running water. "He's just a mechanic. I wonder about all his claims to being a preacher. I'd like to know where he trained to be a minister."

"Maybe if you came along to one of the Sunday family services, Donna, you'd find out," Dad told her, raising his voice to match hers. "Lonn is more than a preacher. He is a real leader. You should see him in action."

"No, thanks," Mom answered. "I'll stick with what I am comfortable with. And I think you should too." Mom still went to the Catholic church with our aunt Jana.

Dad ignored Mom and reached out his hand to pat my shoulder. "You've always been top boys. I know you'll come along and help me out tonight."

"Frank," Mom said from the kitchen, "don't make them go listen to that stuff. They're almost grown-up. Let them make their own choices." She paused for a moment. "Supper's ready. Come eat."

Mom spooned scoops of mashed potatoes into a serving bowl. The bowl looked small in my mom's large hand. She was tall, a couple inches taller than Dad. She could ride a horse as well as anyone. And even though she had always taken care of the cooking and house stuff, there had been nothing she liked better than working outdoors. That seemed to have changed since we moved. She hardly did anything outside the trailer, except her part-time job cleaning rooms at the motel in town. She had grown quiet, as if her spirit was shriveled up. Maybe it was because every time she tried to make a suggestion Dad seemed to get upset. *They are both giving up*, I thought.

David looked envious as Dad put his arm around me. In his overeager voice he told Dad, "I'll say hi to the new guy."

The hot brown smell of hamburger gravy rose in the steam and clung to the vinyl walls. It trickled down in small watery rivulets that, overnight, would freeze.

Dad pressed the mute button on the TV remote. "This is the first break I've gotten since coming here, except for meeting Lonn." He wiped his hands on his jeans as he came to the table. "I'd think you'd be happy about it, Donna."

At sixteen and seventeen David and I were much taller than our dad. Dad was five foot eight and thin like a weathered fence post. Below the short white sleeves of his T-shirt, curving tendons stood out along his arms like gnarled wood. His hair and skin were hardened from working outside.

"It just isn't fair that outsiders are coming into Montana and getting work over people like you," I said. I was thinking of the Triple T. When the new owners took over they wanted to turn it into a fancy vacation ranch and hire people who didn't know the first thing about cattle but looked good sitting on a horse.

"I've got a feeling things are going to change tonight," Dad said.

·CHAPTER TWO·

Sand

At seven o'clock I stood with David and Dad at Lonn's auto repair shop along with two dozen other men. The shop was messy with an oil and gas smell that felt comfortable to me.

Around us men unfolded metal chairs. About the only other young guys at the meeting were Chuck and Travis.

"Hey," I said.

"Campbell," Chuck replied. "I see you're still dragging your brother along."

"He wanted to come," I said. But David stood by himself, not talking to anyone. Even our dad had fallen in with his usual group.

I wanted to keep the conversation with Chuck and Travis going. "I hear there's someone new tonight."

Travis confirmed it. "Lonn keeps them coming."

"It's time to start," I heard Lonn say.

I was hoping that Chuck and Travis would ask me to sit with them. But Chuck said, "Talk to you later." He and Travis took seats on either side of Lonn himself. They looked like bodyguards.

I went over and sat by David. As the others got settled I had trouble sitting still. I always felt weird when Lonn had us pray at the beginning. But it didn't last too long. I looked around the cavernous building. The walls and roof were made of brown sheet metal held together by heavy steel beams. Flags were hanging from the walls: American flags, Montana state flags and some homemade flags with a bleeding cross sewn on them.

As soon as the prayer ended, Lonn started asking questions about what had happened to various people during the week.

"Jack, tell us what you did about your daughter," Lonn said. "Did you tell her she couldn't see that boy again?"

Jack shook his head in frustration. "I told her she was grounded from seeing him. But she don't listen to me."

"God didn't intend for the races to mix, making everyone into mud people," Lonn said. "And since that boy's mother is from Nam, he is impure."

"If you could talk to her," Jack said. "Tell her."

"Be firm. As Guardians of the Identity, we must remain strong in our beliefs. We are here to take a stance." Lonn was already turning his attention to my dad. "How did job hunting go for you this week, Frank?"

I thought this was a strange thing to ask, since Dad had just seen Lonn that morning.

Dad shook his head. "No luck."

"Did you try all of my suggestions?" Lonn's voice was warm.

"Not yet," Dad answered. "But I will."

Lonn nodded to Dad.

He really did sound encouraged, I thought. With one sentence, Lonn could get Dad looking for work, while three days of Mom's pleading wouldn't move him out of his chair.

"We want to welcome a newcomer, Rob Ballard, to Guardians of the Identity," Lonn continued.

"Thanks," Rob said. He looked self-conscious.

"Rob has been to meetings like ours in Idaho. He brings the greetings of the like-minded," Lonn said. "Recently he sold his business there and now he hopes to make a new start in our community."

The men around the room were nodding. Rob looked more relaxed.

"Rob is a witness to the conspirators in Idaho and their infiltrators, funded by Jew-owned banks, who are pushing their way into every part of our region." Lonn spoke in a quiet voice, leaning his elbows on his knees. "It's part of their plan to take over our country."

He held out his hand as if we were all balanced on his palm. I stared at his fingers, stained from working on car engines—

especially the creases, which glared black when he unfolded his hand. He was so intense. His eyes, his face, his whole body radiated what he was saying.

"The Jews and their dark-skinned servants all wear the mark of Satan. They're the Devil's soldiers. And each of you has seen them, in our state, in our town."

I didn't know if I understood everything Lonn said, but I felt myself being drawn toward him. It was almost as if my chair actually inched forward, scraping through the sand that was sprinkled on the floor to cover the grease.

"The Bible foretells it," Lonn continued. "Revelation, chapter thirteen, verse seventeen: 'That no man might buy or sell, save he that has the mark of Satan.' Unless you are in with the Jews, you will be locked out of the marketplace. Rob knows this.

"Tell me," said Lonn. "Are any of you driving forty-thousand-dollar cars, with leather seats and phones? Do any of you own big houses on the hill, looking down on the rest of us?"

In that instant everything became crystal clear. He meant guys like Jason Johnson and our pig landlord. This I could understand. Lonn seemed to know about the kind of trouble David and I had at school. For the first time everything made sense. There was a reason for Dad losing his job. There was a reason for everyone hating us.

Lonn's voice grew louder. "The Jew banks are taking control with their credit cards and computers, making the people slaves with their debt. They're taking over the government in the same way: international loans, trillion-dollar deficit. These are the signs the Bible tells us to look for."

I glanced over at David. As usual, there he was picking at his fingernails, not seeming to listen to a word Lonn was saying. I wanted to shake him. It was no wonder Chuck and Travis didn't like him.

With an abruptness that made me forget David, Lonn was suddenly talking right to me. He sent his words straight into my face. "You are the warrior." I felt what he said like a dry pill inching its way down my throat. I was.

"Together," he went on, "we can halt this advance of the enemy. We might have to start small, digging the dirt out from under their position. But sooner or later we will have dug a pit and they will fall."

I wanted Jason Johnson and the people who bowed down to his kind, like Principal Harrison, to feel the bite. Finally Lonn looked away. But I knew he had more to say to me.

When the meeting finally closed and chairs rattled I headed directly for Lonn. Just as fast Chuck and Travis were standing in front of me, like a door that had to be unlocked.

"Campbell, we've been meaning to talk to you," Travis said in a careful voice.

I kept trying to look beyond them to where Lonn was talking and shaking hands. I saw him put his hand on the new man, Rob. "I want to talk to Lonn." I tried to use a determined voice.

"Then stay awhile," Chuck said. "We're going to meet with him after everybody else leaves."

"Why not now?" I insisted.

"Everybody has to wait their turn," Chuck said. He was dead serious. "You'll be glad if you wait."

The words came floating to me in a haze, pulling me away from Lonn and making me focus on what Chuck was saying. "Yeah?" I asked.

Travis laughed and shared a look with Chuck. "You think Ben would want to come along tonight?"

I was shifting my weight from foot to foot with an eagerness I couldn't hide.

"I think he may," Chuck said.

"Sounds good," I said.

From behind me I felt David join us. Chuck and Travis turned away.

"What were you talking about with those guys?" David asked.

"I'm going to hang around with Chuck and Travis for a while. Help Lonn out," I told David.

He shrugged. "How are you going to get home?"

"Chuck will give me a ride," I said.

"Fine," David said. But I heard the same old jealous anger in his voice. "It can't be any more boring than the meeting was."

"How can you say that?" I was amazed that he didn't get it. "Lonn is right! That's why we're living in a rusting tin can while RETCHes like Jason Johnson get away with beating the crap out of anyone they want."

"It always sounds too much like religious weirdo stuff," David said.

Could David be so dense? The truths were sliding through my brain. "Fine," I said. "I guess that's why Chuck asked me to stay tonight and not you."

David left, angry.

As soon as the last of the men had gone Lonn came to where Chuck, Travis and I waited. He gently put his hand on my shoulder and looked at me the way he had earlier.

"Ben Campbell," he said, smiling. "I'm glad to see you here tonight. I've had my eye on you since you started coming. And I like what I see."

Then he turned to speak to the three of us. "It's time to start letting people know we're here." Lonn handed Chuck a slip of paper. "They wear the mark," he said. "I don't expect anything big. Just something for them to think about. I'll leave the details up to you."

"What do you want us to do?" I didn't know what he was talking about.

"Chuck will fill you in. But . . ." He paused and smiled at me. "These activities must remain strictly within the chosen circle. No one else is to know. You don't want people close to you to get hurt by something they're not ready for. Their time will come. But the strong must lead the way." When he finished, Lonn slid away through a side door.

I wondered what exactly Lonn meant by "their time will come."

Squeezed into Chuck's small car, I watched the moon follow us as if its glazing light were Lonn's words. The car took a long time to warm up, and with the three of us inside, our breath gathered around. Travis scraped ice off the inside of the window as Chuck drove.

We stopped outside a small dark office just west of Main Street. The sign on the front wall read Cohen, Goldberg and Brown.

Chuck announced, "Here we go."

They handed me a can of spray paint and I followed them. In two or three minutes they had painted Jew Pigs and Sucking Kikes in large letters on the door and walls of the building.

Then Chuck took a gas can from the trunk of his Ford and splashed the liquid on a car left parked in front of the office.

21

"Does that car belong to them?" I asked, nodding toward the office.

Chuck shrugged. "It's here, isn't it?" He handed me a book of matches. "Would you like the honor?"

I struck the match and felt its warmth on my hand as I protected the tiny flame. I tossed it gently onto the hood of the car and stepped back in wonder.

·CHAPTER THREE·

Drifts

During the night the wind growled and spit dry snow. I heard it pushing through tree branches and throwing bits of loose junk around outside the trailer. Awake and listening, I thought of that flaming car and the heat against my skin. Making that car burn almost made up for every dirty look, every name hissed at me from under some creep's breath. I could imagine the faces of the rich Jews when they came to work in the morning. I wanted to see it, and even considered skipping school to go. No one would think I was anyone but a passer-by. But then I remembered the in-school detention and knew that if I didn't show up, I would really be in trouble. I was going to have to spend the day in a little room along with David, staring at Jason Johnson's face.

Across from me, David was asleep in his bed. He had the blanket bunched tight around his neck, as if he were hiding from something. He had no idea what Chuck and Travis were into. But I was part of it, finally.

I planned to look for Chuck and Travis before detention. Even though they were too old for school they sometimes hung out in an empty lot across the street. I was eager for new plans.

In the morning when I looked at the clock it was seven-fifteen, late. Through the small window the light was already pasty gray. The wind still blew and I could feel it press on the trailer wall behind me. David's bed was empty. Pushing myself out from under the blankets into the cold room was like pushing against the strong current of a river.

Out in the kitchen I asked Mom, "Where is everyone?"

"Your dad left already. He's going to drop David off at school before meeting Lonn at the café."

"Meeting with Lonn again? That was quick," I said.

"He was so pleased when he came home last night," Mom said. "I think things are going to be better for him."

"You should have gotten me up," I said.

"David mentioned you came in late, so I let you sleep a while longer."

The same restlessness that I had felt the night before rumbled in me. If I was late for school, I wouldn't have time to find Chuck and Travis. Then I would be confined to detention until three o'clock.

"Do you want some eggs?" Mom took slices of bread out of the toaster.

"No time," I said. "I'll take toast with me."

Ten minutes later I was ready and pushed hard against the icy trailer door. As it opened it scraped flat the snow that had built up around the trailer in the short time since Dad and David had left. Outside, the wind tossed handfuls of snow in the air around me. Running to the truck, I couldn't tell if it was still snowing or if the flakes were all windborne.

I was shivering hard, trying to get the truck to start. I could hardly wait to see Chuck and Travis. *Just stay cool,* I told myself. *Don't go looking like a fool in front of them. Don't look too eager.*

I plowed up the hill through the tide of the snowdrifts. In the rearview mirror I saw the wind push snow into the wheel tracks almost as fast as the truck made them. Even with the defroster on high the old Chevy couldn't spit out enough air to warm me.

At the top of the hill the sky behind the mountains was layered pink and yellow. The rocky peaks looked like dark paper silhouettes against new light. I slowed down to take a look at Mason Road. It was just a one-lane shortcut through the fields. It rarely got plowed but I thought if I drove fast enough, I could crash through the drifts. Turning the truck in, I pushed hard over the first rise, sending dry snow flying like a geyser. On the other side of the hill I slammed on the brakes. Blocking the entire road in front of me was a small blue car. Trying to stop suddenly made the truck skid sideways, sending the rear end into the weed-stubbled snow.

What damn fool would drive that puny car on Mason today? I thought. *It doesn't even have four-wheel drive.* I slapped the steering wheel in frustration. The nose of the car was half plunged into a drift. I wasn't going to wait around to find out who the idiot was. I looked on either side of the road for a way around. But we were in a small ravine where steep banks rose on either side.

I put the truck in reverse; the tires spun but the truck stayed still. "Damn it all!" I yelled. Just a hundred yards beyond us the road widened again and had been plowed. But it might as well have been miles instead of yards.

Then I noticed the driver of the blue car standing quietly in the field a few feet from the road. The person gazed out toward the hills, wind whipping the fabric of his or her jacket. The sun was stretching its first fingertips over the surface of polished white.

I got out and started wading through piles of snow. Checking around the smaller vehicle, I tried to see how deep it was stuck. Mentally I measured the distance to the cleared road, wondering if the Chevy could push the little car that far.

"It's so perfect," I heard the person say from deep inside a large parka. I knew it was a girl's voice, and she sounded young. "See how the wind has smoothed everything over, covering all the tracks and scars like a protective blanket. It's a perfect snow." The bulging blue coat arm swept over the field as she spoke.

It was unbelievable that this crazy person who had driven her tiny toy car head-on into a snowbank could stand there talking about the view.

"You know, this really isn't a road," I said.

The girl pushed her hood back and I saw she was about my own age. As she stepped closer to me I was surprised by how tall she was, almost up to my nose. She was as tall as my father.

But before I could even utter one semi-charming line she challenged me. "*You're* driving on this road." She had red-brown hair pulled away from her face and in a braid.

"You're right!" I said with a smile meant to draw her in. "But my truck is twice as big and twice as heavy as your car." To myself I added, *And if you hadn't been in my way, I would have made it.*

She turned away. "I just love the way the snow hides the messes people make. It's like getting a second chance."

The sun rose over the rock edge of the eastern mountains and she raised her hand against the glare. I stared in amazement. Didn't she care that she was blocking my way? "I suggest we think about getting you out or your car will be covered by that snow blanket, and you won't find it again until June."

"I drive this way because from this spot you can't see anything but light and snow and rocks," she went on as if she hadn't heard me. "No house, no town, nothing out of place."

"Except for your stranded car," I added.

"The road was okay yesterday," she said.

"The wind's been blowing all night," I told her. "And the road is lower here, so the snow gathers here and gets packed down."

"I think I figured that out," the girl said. "But thanks for telling me."

"With chains on my truck I might be able to push you out."

She looked me over then. "Great," she said.

As she grinned I couldn't help thinking that she wasn't pretty, but there was something about her face I liked. Even with the smart mouth.

She walked beside me, talking as I went to get the shovel out of the truck. "Do you go to school in town? We just moved here from Michigan a couple of months ago. My parents built a house out on Lancy Road, down by the river. It's my mom's dream house. She always wanted to live in the country. It is beautiful compared to Flint. My mom's a nurse and my dad's starting a new company. He also works as an economic consultant until he gets the new business going."

She talked all the way to the truck and back. I didn't have to say a thing, so I just tried to look strong.

"Do you always keep a shovel in your truck?" she asked me. This time she waited for me to answer.

I leaned on the handle, breathing hard. "Are you sure you're not from Mars instead of Flint? This is Montana. Everyone should carry a shovel, especially people who drive their cars fifty yards from any real road."

The girl laughed. "You have to admit this is the prettiest place in the whole area. You can see every mountain for miles." She spread her arms out wide and spun around.

I suddenly realized I was smiling back at her for real. This was near my favorite place too, the hill where it felt like I could take off flying.

After I finished clearing the snow from around the front of her car and putting chains on the rear wheels of the truck, I told her to get into her car. "Go slow but steady. I'll push from behind. Just don't slam on the brakes!"

It didn't take long for her car to come free. She stopped when we reached the plowed road and came over to me.

"Thanks a lot for helping me," she said. "By the way, my name's Eden Taylor."

"It was a pleasure rescuing you, Eden Taylor," I said.

"Do you have a name?" she teased. "Or should I just call you My Hero if I see you again?"

"Being stuck in weather like this is no joke," I said more seriously. "You can get into trouble out here in winter. People have frozen to death in their cars." I stopped when I saw she was about to break up laughing. Somehow when she teased, it didn't feel like an insult.

"I am truly grateful," Eden said. "And I promise I will only drive on real roads from now on. But I would like to know if you have a name."

"Ben Campbell."

"Ben. Short for Benjamin?"

"Yes, ma'am." I bowed with exaggerated politeness.

"Well, Ben, maybe I'll see you at school?" She said it as a question. She took off her coat and threw it on the backseat.

She did have a nice build.

"I'm usually there. Unless someone is blocking the road."

"Then I'll see you sometime." She quickly jumped into her car and started in the direction of town.

For a moment I let myself enjoy the view. I'd earned it by digging her damned car out. I wondered if she really wanted to see me again. She had freckles spreading across her cheeks. But it was her green eyes that held me.

Wet and shivering, I followed in my truck.

By the time I arrived there was no sign of Chuck and Travis. Only ten minutes until classes began and I was to report to detention.

There were a lot of kids here I still didn't recognize. I hadn't remembered seeing Eden before, but after that morning I saw her everywhere. The first time was while I stood at my locker. My hands were still cold from all that shoveling. She came down the hall with two other girls.

"Hey, it's my hero," she said loudly.

"It's the damsel in distress." I showed her my red fingers. "Thanks to you taking the scenic route, I think I have frostbite."

She laughed and told her friends how I had saved her from freezing to death just that morning.

Later, when David and I were released from the detention room to eat, I saw her in the cafeteria. She waved to me from a table.

"Who's that?" David asked.

Jason Johnson, standing in line next to us, saw her and said, "Mmm, tight."

I didn't answer. Maybe I had to sit in a small room with him but I didn't have to talk to him.

All morning Jason had tried making conversation. He was still trying. "Great game last week, huh?"

I scowled at him.

"Look, Campbell," he said. "I'm sorry I punched your brother. But every day in history class the punk keeps kicking the back of my chair, no matter how often I tell him to cut it out. Then yesterday, when we're walking out of class, he sneers, 'Your chair's got the shakes, or are you playing with yourself?' So I smacked him."

I knew that was just the kind of thing David would do. But I wasn't going to give Johnson the satisfaction of knowing I agreed with him. So I stayed silent and Johnson gave it up.

When Johnson finally quit trying to talk to me, I had plenty of time to think about Eden. Her face and voice grew in my mind until she seemed to float there all the time.

After school David and I were headed for the truck when I noticed Chuck at the far end of the parking lot by his car. There were several other kids with him.

"David, wait for me in the truck. I want to talk with Chuck over there."

"What about me? Why do I have to wait in the truck?"

"Come on, David," I said. "I'll make it up to you somehow." Wasn't I always doing things for my brother? I had just saved him from RETCH Jason Johnson, after all.

Reluctantly David walked on and I went over to Chuck.

"Campbell," Chuck called as I approached. He stepped away from the group he was with. Then he gripped my arm, grinning. "I looked for you this morning. Travis and I took a drive past our little job to see how it turned out."

"Detention," I explained.

"Wish you could have been there," he went on. "Cops all over the place. And some pitiful scrawny kike in a suit trying to scrub the walls. It was great."

"What about the car?" I asked him. I felt the excitement in my throat.

"A black shell."

"I want to do it again," I said.

"Sure," Chuck assured me.

But his answer wasn't enough. "When?"

"Hang on," he said. "You got to stay quiet for a few days. Let the newspaper cover this one. Do too much and each job won't get the attention it deserves."

I noticed David giving me impatient looks from the truck. Chuck followed my gaze and said, "I'll be talking to you." And then he was gone, melting into his group.

I was left standing alone. This new hunger cramped at my insides. I wanted the previous night's feeling of power again, *soon*.

·CHAPTER FOUR·

Metal

Thanksgiving came and went. For more than two weeks I waited for Chuck to give me news from Lonn. I saw him several times after school and at the meetings. But nothing was said about burning the car or when we would go again.

"You have to understand, Campbell," Chuck explained. "Let

everybody stew about it awhile. Then when the fuss is about to die down, *bam,* we do it again."

"Yeah, I get it," I told him. But it didn't quiet the urge to feel that power again.

I hung on until the next Friday. That was the day I saw Eden in the library. I had gone in to pick up a computer printout for the English teacher. Eden was in there sitting around a table with a couple of girls that I hadn't seen her with before. I knew the blond girl next to her from math. Her name was Jill. She seemed the type to hang out with a RETCH like Jason Johnson.

"Hello, Lady Eden." I walked past and Eden waved. I almost stopped to talk more but Jill elbowed Eden and leaned over to her, whispering. Her eyes skimmed over my body. I could feel it. Standing at the counter, I asked the librarian for the printout. I kept my back to the girls but could still feel their looks. It was like being back in Prairie Springs, when girls admired me all the time.

"It's yummy from this angle," Jill said loud enough for me to hear. "But it was better when he still wore those butt-tight cowboy jeans."

"Jill!" Eden gave a shocked laugh.

The librarian took her time finding the papers and so I leaned on the counter and ventured a look over to the table. I thought this might turn out to be fun. Jill's hungry looks made me tingle and feel every inch of my body. I saw Eden blushing as Jill whispered to her again.

Eden said, "I met him a couple weeks ago."

Then suddenly Jill's voice rose intentionally. "He's the one who got in a fight with Jason." Her tone took on a cold edge but she was still giving me that hungry look.

"He seems nice," Eden said. But it was almost a question.

"Nice to see, but not to be seen with," Jill said.

The bitch! Then I knew what was really happening. She had me pinned. That girl had turned me on and was now deliberately cutting me open. Staring at me, she continued, barely bothering to whisper. "Trashy. Lives in some dump of a trailer."

Eden's face was bright red and she wouldn't look at me.

"Girl, you don't want to go out in a pickup that stinks like cow crap!" Jill concluded.

I wanted to close her ugly mouth with my fist. When the librarian finally handed me the printout I grabbed it from her. Jill smiled as she watched me turn red and fumble in my anger. And I couldn't think of a thing to say. I just walked out cursing Jill, cursing Eden for turning out to be another RETCH and cursing myself for not saying anything to them.

I was headed back to English class when Eden came up behind me. "Ben, wait."

I stopped but couldn't face her. She put her hand on my arm and for a second I didn't know whether I was going to take a punch at her or start crying. It was such a rush of different feelings. I tried to suck everything deep inside, like taking a huge breath of freezing air.

"I'm sorry about what Jill said. She isn't usually mean," Eden explained.

When I felt I had my face fixed into a don't-care look I turned to her. "That kind of mean takes practice," I said. "She gets an A-plus in Rich Bitch class."

"I guess she is a snob," Eden said. "But I've only been here since school started. I made friends with whoever let me. It's not easy being new."

"At least people let you make friends with them," I snapped.

"I don't care what she said about you."

"You'd better care," I said. "Friends like that can make life hell for you if you cross them." She looked embarrassed again. I didn't wait around to hear any more lame excuses. I could see what was going on. She wouldn't be wasting time talking to me in the future.

After school I was still fuming. It was like being hungry for hours and not getting any food. My stomach cramped and ached. I couldn't sit still or rid my mind of that scene in the library. I had to do something, anything, to get it out of me.

In the parking lot I saw Chuck sitting on the hood of his car. "Hey, Campbell." He beckoned me over. "Lonn wants us. It's time to make ourselves seen again."

Hot damn! This could be what I needed. I didn't want Chuck to see I was so excited. "Sounds good."

Then my brother joined us. "What's up?"

I didn't know what Chuck's reaction to David would be. In the past he had ignored him. But that day I was surprised when Chuck said with friendliness, "We're cooking up some plans for tonight."

I saw David hesitate. Neither of us knew if this was an invitation or not.

Chuck turned to me. "Why don't you bring your brother, Campbell."

I shrugged and said, "Sure."

"Eight o'clock at Lonn's." Chuck drove off.

In the truck David's eyes were shining. "So what are we doing tonight? Is there a game on TV?"

"I don't know what we'll do," I answered truthfully. But I knew it wouldn't be watching TV. I had to wonder if David was up for what Chuck really had in mind.

As we pulled into the driveway I saw a little Toyota parked in front. "Aunt Jana's here," I said.

"At the same time as Dad?" David pointed to the other truck. "I wonder if the blood is flowing yet."

Aunt Jana is our mom's sister. She's lived in Lodgette ever since she got her nursing degree. Now she works at the hospital. She kind of likes rubbing it in that she was the first and only person in the family to get a college degree. She had always bugged Dad, but since he lost his job he couldn't stand her.

"Hey!" Aunt Jana greeted us as we came in the door. She was leaning on the kitchen counter with a cup of coffee in her hands.

"Hi, Aunt Jana," I returned. I looked around for Dad. He was sitting in his chair. He didn't turn around.

"What do you boys say to Christmas dinner at my house in town?" Aunt Jana asked. My aunt's face looked a lot like my mom's, but Aunt Jana was more outspoken. She didn't hesitate to say exactly what she was thinking. When she talked to my dad he never knew if she was kidding or really giving him a hard time. But he wasn't quick enough to tease her back, so he just got mad.

Dad grumbled something that I couldn't hear.

"Yeah, we hear you over there," Aunt Jana said to Dad. "You have to get out of that chair sometime. It might as well be to eat at my house."

My mom gave the back of Dad's head a sad look and said, "That would be nice, Jana, thanks."

"Maybe we can even get the folks out from Miles City. Besides, you couldn't fit a turkey into this place," Aunt Jana said, looking around the trailer.

After Aunt Jana left, Dad started in. "That woman should watch her tongue. No wonder she can't get a man to marry her."

When David and I arrived at the auto shop the lights were off. Out in the cold night, Lonn was talking with Chuck and Travis. They stood in a huddle with hands in their pockets and bounced as they talked, rocking toe to heel as if trying to push the cold away. When we pulled up Lonn headed for his truck.

Chuck came to my window. "You guys ready for a little fun?"

Like a young puppy, David chimed in, "Absolutely."

He didn't have a clue what we were going to do but he was almost jumping up and down on the seat. I could see Chuck giving him an annoyed look.

"Why don't you guys come in my car," Chuck suggested.

We drove toward town. Looking out the window, I caught sight of a street sign glowing in the headlights. Lancy Road. I thought of Eden and wondered what she was doing. It made all the anger at her and Jill come surging back through me like a wave.

To take my mind off it I asked, "Where are we going?"

Travis twisted around to us. "Several tasty spots have been suggested."

"Jew hunting," Chuck said. "Always an open season."

David gave me a questioning glance. I ignored it. I wasn't going to let my little brother spoil the action.

Travis handed back a six-pack and I took a beer before passing it to David. He gave me another one of those looks.

"Come on, David," I said. "You're going to have to do it sometime. All the guys drink after the football games."

Chuck suddenly laughed and said to David, "Still the little kid, huh?" That got David mad. He flipped the can open and started gulping. After a few minutes he started on a second one.

A few blocks from the center of town Chuck parked the car where bare-branched trees hid us. He pointed to one of the houses. It was completely dark. I knew no one lived in it.

"It's the Jew church," Chuck said. "We need to leave them a little message." He opened the trunk and took out the cans of spray paint.

"Like the other night?" I asked hopefully. But there wasn't a car close enough to set on fire.

"Not exactly," he answered. "First we write our message and then we'll give you the special calling card."

"But we have to be quick," Travis said. "Too many houses here to hang around for long."

I turned to the car. "Hey, David, you coming?"

"Yeah," David mumbled as he pulled himself out of the backseat. But he just kind of stood there not moving. He looked like one of those toy blow-up punching bags, the kind you hit and they bounce back up. No wonder Jason Johnson punched him. Chuck and Travis exchanged exasperated looks.

My brother was a constant embarrassment. "I told you to go easy on the beers, David," I said.

He groaned and let his body fall back across the seat of Chuck's car. "I feel dizzy."

"Never mind." Chuck handed me a can of paint. "He's extra baggage anyway."

Before closing the trunk, Chuck took out a .22 rifle, the kind David and I learned to shoot with when we were kids, back at the ranch. "This speaks louder than words," he said, handing me the gun.

The metal barrel was freezing cold from being in the trunk. I couldn't hold it in my bare hands so I pulled the sleeves of my jacket down to grip it.

"Let's hurry," Travis said. He started across the street toward the house.

"And stick together." Chuck looked right at me.

Chuck and Travis painted Nazi swastikas and Kill Kikes in large dripping orange letters across the front of the house. Then they turned to me. "Let her rip, Campbell," Chuck said.

I felt the rifle in my hands and it was the same sense of power I'd had when I threw the match onto the car. Even better. I opened fire and felt the exploding power of each bullet as it left the gun. No one could be stronger than I was at that moment. My fingers pulsed and I felt the heat spread through my body. The hot metal shells struck the building with a quiet shattering of wood and the sharp crash of glass. I got off five shots before a light came on a few houses away.

Chuck elbowed me as a signal. As we ran to the car I felt my legs surge with strength. I could have run for miles and miles without even feeling it. Chuck was already pulling away from the curb as I pushed David's sagging body farther into the car and slammed the door.

A few blocks away Chuck announced, "Gentlemen, that was perfect."

"Yes!" I cried, and slammed the back of the seat with my fist, trying to express more of the release. It was like a flash flood racing over the surface of my skin.

"So, Campbell," Travis said, laughing, "you like the gun?"

I nodded.

·CHAPTER FIVE·

Weight

We drove around for about a half hour longer, drinking and shouting out the excitement we all felt. Everyone except David. He sat quietly staring at his knees. But my feelings of strength started fading too soon. No matter how hard I tried to stay pumped up, I couldn't. And as it all slipped away like a slow leak in a tire, I found, underneath, that I was still mad. So when David said, "I think we should go home," I lit into him.

"You piss-ass," I said.

Chuck interrupted me. "We're not done yet."

"No way!" Travis added. "There is more fun to be had."

My brother sulked as I whispered, "Come on, David. This is what you've been wanting, isn't it? You gotta stand up for yourself for once. Fight instead of sneaking kicks at the back of other guys' chairs."

I could see David puff out in shock at what I knew. "Screw you, Ben," he growled at me. "I didn't do anything to Johnson."

I wanted to egg him on more. I thought it would make him tough. Chuck handed him another beer, which I didn't think was such a good idea. But he said, "Come on, Dave. Lonn said he wanted you to be with us tonight."

I looked at Chuck in surprise and he nodded at me. I tried to go along with it. "Yeah, we don't want Lonn to be disappointed. Not when he's helping Dad out." I said it even though the words sounded hollow and meaningless in my mouth. But David was giving in. He was always trying to please Dad, even though he could never quite get the knack of it.

We drove into the nice neighborhoods that were on the outskirts of town. Finally Chuck pulled over and turned off the engine. Everyone spent a moment in silence. Then Chuck pointed to a white house four doors down from where we were parked. "You know who lives there?" He grinned.

"Nope," I said.

"Faggot Trenton Biggs," Chuck and Travis almost said together.

"Who's that?" David asked.

"He goes to your school," Chuck said.

"How do you know he's queer?" I asked. I knew who they were talking about. A tall quiet guy with wispy hair that was almost white. He never said much and hung around mostly with girls.

"The guy has it written all over him. He wiggles his butt like a girl, he talks like a girl and he wants to be a girl," Chuck said.

"He wants into guys' pants," Travis added.

"I've seen him around," David said.

"But what's he got to do with anything even if he is a fag?" I questioned.

"He's just another kind we don't want around here. Who knows what he's doing—or *who* he's doing," Travis said, laughing.

The street was well lit, so we left the car a good block away, under some spruce trees that shaded it from view. Cutting through the yards, Chuck warned us to stay quiet. As we neared the Biggses' house we ducked back behind a row of bushes. I could see there were lights on inside. Most of the curtains were drawn shut except for over a large picture window in the living room.

Chuck reached down and dug around in the snow until he found a rock. Travis threw his beer can on the ground and started digging too. He handed a large stone to David and one to me.

I gripped the rock. It fit well in my hand. I knew this stone could absorb all the energy that ached inside me. I thought about Eden and Jill in the library, about all the crap I had to listen to from people like them. In his big house Trenton Biggs was just as bad as any RETCH.

Chuck and Travis were whispering to David. "Send that rock to hell, boy! Throw it!"

David just stared at the rock in his hand.

"For once in your life, David, don't be a wimp," I said. "Remember RETCH Johnson." As he looked up at me I pulled back and threw my rock. Chuck and Travis followed my action. Finally David did as well.

I watched my rock travel through the cold air. It was like part of me went with it: particles of dirt, and cells of skin shed from my hand. It carried my message. I heard the window shattering and could almost feel the glass shower over my own body, as if I had flung myself instead of the stone.

Then I heard screams from the house and more lights started to come on. The yellow brightness flooded the yard. Chuck and Travis shouted, "Come on!" and took off running with David toward the car. I started to follow but then I glanced at the people now visible in the window and froze. Two adults, upset and shouting, bent over the mess. The man clutched one of the rocks in his hand. But it was the face of Trenton Biggs, his pale hair and skin glowing from the house light, that carved itself into my brain. It was a solemn, surprisingly calm face, the same angerless, accepting expression he wore at school. His delicate features were framed in jagged glass. Small eyes pointed directly at me. I was pretty sure he couldn't see me through the darkness, but I felt his stare like an electric current. It was as if he knew who was out there. But he couldn't. I tried to shake free of the connection that gripped me.

Suddenly the face in the window was David's, watching me sneak away with Dad to go fishing without him. But he had seen us and watched with an empty gaze. Trenton's face held the same look. He knew the rock was meant for him and, without being told with words, he knew why.

The next thing I was aware of was David beside me grabbing at my sleeve. "Run! We have to get out of here," he whispered. I heard Chuck's car in the distance and felt my brother leave me. But still I couldn't move.

It wasn't until the two adults dragged Trenton away from the window that I started running. Chuck's car was gone, so I turned and took off in the direction of town.

For more than an hour I walked. Sticking to dark streets, I wound through the quiet neighborhoods of Lodgette. What had happened back there? Why had I seized up, as if Trenton Biggs's eyes were a harness around my neck? Now the same feeling followed me like a shadow, but a shadow that had weight.

I didn't feel the power I had when we burned the car or shot into the Jew church. I kept thinking it was because Chuck had taken off and left me in the cold. It made me angry that I didn't have any idea where Chuck, Travis and my brother had gone, except that they hadn't bothered to wait for me. More anger to add to the rest. And this time it got worse instead of being the release I had longed for.

I moved fast, pumped by the hard, cold air sitting on my shoulders and the heavy rage in my stomach. I kept my hands deep in my pockets and hunched my neck down in my jacket, trying to stay warm.

In the dark I ran into a mailbox mounted on a wood post. I kicked it then, over and over, as if I could beat the life out of it. But soon I got scared that someone would hear me and I ran.

After another ten minutes I knew I had to find someplace to get out of the cold. I walked past Aunt Jana's house and looked at the warmth of her lights squeezing through drawn drapes. It would be a relief to tell someone what had happened that night. My aunt Jana was honest and blunt, but she was always easy to talk to—maybe because she wasn't afraid to tell you exactly what her opinion was, and you always knew she still cared in spite of it.

I was almost ready to knock on the door when I realized that, as pissed as I was, Aunt Jana would know something was wrong, no matter what story I tried to give her. She would report to Mom. And Mom would tell Dad. I knew for certain. I turned back into the cold.

After another half a block my aching fingers told me to break a garage or car window to get out of the cold. I had already turned in the direction of the alley when I heard a car slowing down behind me.

"Ben, where have you been?" It was Travis's voice. "Mr. Power, soldier boy, get in this car," he shouted.

My foot kicked aside some beer cans as I slid into the back beside David. Inside, their hot breath smelled of alcohol and smoke. My iced skin stung as if I were being slapped all over my body. My limbs began to throb from the heat. David was hunched over, drinking another beer.

My mouth was so stiff with cold I couldn't speak. David's silence made me nervous. What was he thinking about? Or was he just drunk? I found myself staring at him, trying to see Trenton's face from the window in my brother. I had to make myself stop.

As if Chuck were reading my thoughts, he said, "Damn it, Ben, what happened back there?"

"Nothing happened." I forced my jaw to move, feeling my anger break like sweat through my body's shivering. "Except you guys took off without me."

"What do you mean, we took off? Your brother there couldn't drag you away," Chuck said. "He's been whining ever since."

"I didn't want to leave you," David said quietly from his hunched position. I thought his words sounded slurred.

"Thanks, David," I said.

"Thanks?" Chuck started to shout. "You could have gotten us all caught. Lonn expects this to go right every time. We land in jail and everything's ruined."

"What's everything?" David asked. No one answered him.

I didn't exactly know what everything was but I was catching on. To Chuck, Travis and Lonn this wasn't about just getting kicks and feeling big. There was something more. It felt like they had a plan. A plan that snaked around me in cold shivers.

"Hey, it was only for a second." As I said the words I knew I was conceding, and I hated Chuck for that. After I had been so hot for action the last two weeks.

Chuck's voice was calm again. "We've got to work together. If one goes down, it's the end."

"I don't see what is so important about a few rocks through a window," I said. "It's not as good as burning the car or shooting up the other place."

That was it, I had decided. That was why I hadn't felt that same surge of energy as I had the first two times. Just breaking a window was lame.

"What car?" David asked.

"Oh, nothing." I didn't want to explain it to him.

"Lonn doesn't think so," Chuck said.

"I don't give a shit what Lonn thinks," I said.

Chuck turned in the seat and stared hard into my face. "You'd better," he said. His voice was ultracalm, in complete control.

I felt a twinge of fear. But before I could think of any reply Travis cut in. "Come on, Ben, it was kick-ass tonight."

David was bent over and didn't seem to be listening. Suddenly he spoke out. "Stop the car! I'm going to be sick."

Chuck pulled the car off onto the gravel roadside and my brother opened his door to puke. He couldn't get out, but just leaned over. After a few minutes he groaned and wiped his mouth. The smell of vomit hung over us like a damp fog. How could the night start out so great and end so bad? My feelings swirled around me in confusion, just like the smell.

"The kid can't hold beer, can he?" Chuck said.

"I'll take him home," I said.

Chuck stared straight ahead. "Fine with me, Campbell." He drove back to Lonn's shop and our truck.

·CHAPTER SIX·

Heat

The next day, Saturday, David didn't get out of bed until after twelve. I wasn't surprised. The night before, he'd hardly been able to stay on his feet. I almost had to carry him into the house.

He kept crying, "Don't let go of me, Ben. Everything's spinning."

I was really glad the folks were asleep and I didn't have to do any explaining. I helped him onto his bed and pulled off his boots. Finally, as I sat by him, his face went slack and relaxed into sleep. I remembered again how bad I had felt the time we didn't take him fishing with us. I pushed the hair out of his face before moving away. "I still look out for you," I whispered.

That next morning, before David even dragged himself out of bed, I already had a pile of wood split and stacked. Once I got going, I liked chopping wood. It's the feeling of being warm from exercise while standing out in the cold.

David stuck a sour face out the door and stared at me.

"Looking fine this morning," I said to him.

"Mom says to come eat your lunch," he grumbled. "And we have to talk later."

Now I'll hear it, I thought. *I'll find out what David was thinking about last night.* For a split second I thought he might rat on us to the police, but then I knew that no matter what he thought, my brother would never turn me in.

I went inside. Mom was putting grilled cheese sandwiches on plates, as usual a bit blackened around the edges. Greasy smoke dimmed the room and made breathing hard after having been outside.

"Aren't you eating, David?" I poked at him.

"David's got a stomach bug today," our mom said sympathetically.

"Gee, I hope it's not contagious," I said.

He gave me an angry look through watery eyes.

Dad took a big bite of sandwich and opened the paper. "Look at this. Someone is out to get the Jews." He held up a newspaper photo of the vandalized church.

For an instant I was afraid the article would also mention Trenton's house. I don't know why I even thought about it. But when I looked, it was just the empty Jew church.

Then I noticed David squirming beside me. I felt panic. *He's going to start squealing right in front of Mom and Dad,* I thought.

But when I looked over to David he was looking back at me with a sly little smile on his face!

Dad went right on talking, not seeing our looks. "Maybe them Jews will start to see that they don't belong here."

"Yeah," David agreed. "We won't let the RETCHes and all those mudskins get the better of us."

"Destroying a church!" Mom was shocked. "That is terrible. You can't believe that is any way to solve a problem, Frank."

"I didn't say that," Dad said. "I just think we should all stick to our own kind. Jews with Jews, whites with whites."

"You don't even know anyone but 'your own kind.'" Mom stressed the last three words. "So how can you say you wouldn't like them as well as anybody else? Or even recognize a Jewish person if you met one?"

"We'll know plenty of those kikes and mudskins if we let them move in and take over like they want," David said.

"That is enough of that kind of talk," Mom said to David. "I won't have it in my house. Where could you get such ideas?"

Dad looked embarrassed. But he didn't tell Mom that the ideas were coming from Lonn. So I stepped in, trying to change the subject.

"Think you'll have time for some fishing this afternoon?" I asked Dad.

"Maybe." He went back to reading his paper.

It was lunchtime on Monday when Eden found me in the cafeteria. "Ben." She sat down beside me. "I haven't been able to forget about what Jill did on Friday in the library."

As she spoke I realized I wasn't angry with Eden anymore. Jill had used us both.

"Forget it," I said.

"I phoned Jill," Eden explained. "I told her I thought it was a really mean thing to do and that I didn't see anything wrong with being friends with you."

"What did she say?" I couldn't help asking.

"Not much," Eden said. "But I don't think she's interested in having me for a friend anymore."

I felt her hand on my arm asking for my reaction. I wasn't sure what I felt. She was taking a risk for me. I knew that. But I wasn't sure I really wanted her to. Her hand tingled where it touched my shirt, almost like feathers from a tiny bird sweeping past my arm. I tried to think of something to say but nothing came out.

Finally she said, "My mom says I am way too forward for my own good. But why haven't you ever asked me out? I met you more than a month ago, and I know you don't have a girlfriend. And I'm sure having to defend myself as if I were really dating you."

"Maybe Jill was right. Maybe you shouldn't be seen with me," I answered.

"Thanks for telling me now," she teased. "Look, it doesn't have to be much. Coffee after school one day? Wednesday?"

That was when I saw Trenton. He lumbered through the cafeteria door, slumped and expressionless. My first reaction was to slide under the table so he wouldn't notice me. But he walked by without a glance. My body felt hot, as if I were feverish.

"What are you staring at?" Eden watched my face.

I found myself touching my hot cheeks, my fingers points of ice against the skin. "Do you know him?" I indicated Trenton with my head.

"Sure," Eden said still puzzled. "He's in my English class."

"Is he . . ." I hesitated, not knowing exactly how she felt about things like that. "Is he, you know, gay?"

"How should I know?" Eden was surprised and obviously embarrassed. "He's smart. He's a really good writer. He read one of his stories for the class. Why do you want to know if he's gay?"

"Someone told me he was, that's all."

"From the look on your face I thought maybe he'd come on to you or something," she teased. "Is that why you won't go out with me, Ben?"

"No way!" Every masculine urge in me came to my defense. "I mean, I do want to go out with you."

Laughing, she said, "Good. I'll hold you to Wednesday, then." She got up from the table and I watched her walk away.

When Wednesday came, I realized I was excited about seeing Eden that afternoon. I was standing at my locker just letting anticipation splash around me when I caught sight of her. As soon as I saw the long reddish braid go bouncing down the hall I knew it was Eden. Everything else on either side of her seemed to grow fuzzy, while each tiny detail about her became clear: white sweater, black jeans, the end of her braid held together with a black elastic band, small gold earrings shaped like crescent moons swinging from her ears.

"Ben!" I suddenly heard David's voice right next to me. "What planet are you on?"

"What?" I asked.

"Chuck sent me to find you. We can hang out, then he'll give us a ride to the meeting."

"Chuck sent you?" I was surprised that Chuck would even bother with David after he had been such a wimp the other night.

"Yeah." I could see the anger grow on my brother's face, as if he knew what I was thinking. He added, "I saw him out in the parking lot. He's waiting for us."

Just then Eden showed up. "Hi, Ben. Hi, Ben's brother."

David just barely nodded to Eden, then stared at his feet. He was unbelievably shy around girls. He seemed to turn into a big, stumbling goon.

"You ready to go?" she asked me.

I saw David look surprised and excluded. And I was stuck again. I fumbled with a couple pennies in my pocket, trying to think of what to do. Go with David and Chuck, or go with Eden? But the pull of the guys, like a craving, was too strong.

"Something's come up," I told her. "I can't go."

"Oh?"

I felt really bad, not just because I did want to go out with her but because she had given up her friendship with the rich kids to do it. Behind Eden, light from the large glass door bounced off her back, lighting her hair and putting her face into golden shadows. It was as if she glowed. I was about to change my mind and skip going to Lonn's when I saw Chuck drive up to the door. He honked the horn.

"We gotta go," David begged. "We need to scope out a few things for Lonn. You know what I mean."

I felt my brother's plea in both look and stance. "We can do it another day, can't we?" I asked Eden.

"I guess so," Eden said. She turned in the direction I was looking and asked, "Who's that?"

But before I could answer, David tugged on my sleeve and I left.

When we arrived at Lonn's it was obvious that Chuck had already told him about Friday night and he was pleased. He greeted us with smiles and claps on the back.

"I told you this was going to be good," Chuck said. I looked at him and was shocked to see he was talking to David instead of to me. I turned away and continued setting up chairs for the meeting.

Soon men started to fill the room. The many bodies heated the air until the area near the inner circle of chairs, those closest to the heater, became too warm. Hot air rushed out of the oil stove and everyone peeled off layers of jackets, hats, gloves and sweaters. But I could see the ice built up around the outer edges of the building. It started at the base of the small windows and crept down the corrugated metal walls to the concrete floor.

The meeting started with Lonn saying the same prayer that I now knew by heart. "God of Adam, purify us and fill us with your strength. Teach us to recognize the enemy within our midst and give us the courage to struggle against their corruptions. Amen." Right away he rose to speak.

Beside me David listened with rapt attention. *This is a switch,* I thought. *For once my brother is involved and I am the one just sitting here.*

When he saw me looking at him he leaned over and whispered, "Lonn is going to make an announcement about the job we did Friday night."

"How do you know that?" I asked.

"Chuck told me," he answered.

"Where's Dad?" I whispered. "Why isn't he here tonight?"

"Shh, I want to listen," he said.

My surprise must have shown, because David looked smug as he turned his attention back to Lonn. Thoughts kept whirling around me. *Chuck told him we would be recognized tonight? When did this happen and where was I?* Suddenly I was the one who felt left out and stupid.

As I was trying to figure out what was going on David elbowed me and I heard Lonn say, "This week we have cause to celebrate. We recognize the bravery and initiative of four boys who have taken the first step into manhood."

So David was right.

"They have pledged themselves to the cause and in so doing have become the protectors of our future. Our homeland is in their strong hands," Lonn said. "They will ensure us a home for our descendants. A white home. A pure home."

Lonn's speech hit me. He talked and talked but never said anything specific. It sounded as if he were telling what we did, but he didn't. He also made us sound as if we were doing something good and positive. No spray paint, no car burning and no guns were mentioned. It made me feel that what we had done was actually stupid. I was glad our dad wasn't there. Then his voice rose to a shout that made me jump.

"We whites are God's true children! We will no longer tolerate the pollution of our place by Jews and their colored followers."

In my mind again was Trenton's face, surrounded by the shattered window, taking over all my thoughts. It was like a bad song that you can't stop humming. And for some reason I was totally embarrassed by what Lonn was saying. It wasn't different from any other time but now I could feel all the eyes focus my way. I had liked the meeting better when I was just part of an audience, as invisible as the guys around me. Now the room felt tight and airless. It was like I couldn't get a breath into my lungs.

At the time it had felt so kick-ass good to shoot that rifle at the walls of the Jew place, but I didn't want anyone to know about it, especially Mom and Dad. Besides, that night sure hadn't ended so great, with us breaking that stupid window and me freezing at seeing Trenton.

A change in the tone of Lonn's voice brought my attention back to what was happening. "Let's now recognize and thank these young men: Chuck Lamb, Travis Mackey, David and Ben Campbell."

There was scattered applause and voices called out, "Yes!"

I wanted to disappear under my seat. But David, Mr. Timid, was sitting up tall, his face glowing. This even though he hadn't done anything except drink too much and sulk!

As the meeting closed I asked David again why Dad wasn't at the meeting that night.

"He's training for his new job," David answered.

"What job?" I asked.

"At the Quick Mart," David said. "The one owned by the new guy, Rob."

All my discomfort burned in me like a smoldering fire. "He better not find out what we did. He'd throw a fit and I don't even want to think about what Mom would do."

"How do you know?" David asked. "He agrees that those kind of people shouldn't be allowed to live here."

"Maybe, but that's different from knowing your kids broke the law," I said. "And he sure didn't say anything to Mom when she asked where we were getting our ideas."

I wondered if Dad suspected that we were involved with the vandalism. He had looked uncomfortable when Mom was giving her opinion. Maybe he knew more than he wanted to admit. Would he blind himself in order to get a job out of Lonn? Even with all the bad things I had done recently, I didn't want to believe my father would do anything but what was right.

As usual, Chuck and Travis were gatekeepers for Lonn. "What do you need, Campbell?" It was as if Chuck were asking for a password to enter.

"What's Lonn doing announcing to everyone what we did? Someone here could squeal to the cops."

"I didn't hear anything about Friday," Chuck said, almost laughing. He turned to Travis. "Did you?"

Travis shook his head.

"They're going to figure it out," I said. "What if my dad had been here? I don't want my parents knowing."

"Then you better make sure they don't find out. Besides, Lonn knows how far to go," Travis warned. "He's a pro."

That was true. Lonn knew where to stop in order to keep himself guilt-free. *We* were now criminals, not him. I went back to David, who was waiting by the door. "Let's go," I said.

As we were leaving, Chuck walked over and held me aside for a second. "If word gets out about us to the wrong people, we'll know where the weak link is, Campbell. And you wouldn't want your dad to lose his new job."

Once we were in our truck David said, "That was great, wasn't it? Wahoo!" he whooped.

"Yeah," I agreed. I thought of Chuck's last threat, and all I could do was press my fist against my gut where the fear and guilt had taken root.

·CHAPTER SEVEN·

Sweat

The next morning the weather had turned warmer. As dawn faded in I heard the metallic pinging sound of water dripping on the roof of the trailer. Damp smells of cooking and coffee oozed into our room from under the door. It wasn't unusual to have a December warm spell, and I savored getting dressed with fingers that weren't stiff with cold.

I had spent much of the night thinking about what had happened at the meeting. I was scared. Even though I knew Lonn was behind everything we did, I felt he could claim innocence and turn on David and me if we did anything that displeased him.

David heard me moving around and started to stir under the covers. Before his head was even all the way out I said, "I've been thinking about Lonn."

"I was thinking about everybody applauding us." David gave a sleepy smile.

"No," I went on. "I don't think it's such a good idea to be Lonn's hit men."

David sat straight up in bed. "Are you calling me a fool? You're the one who was all hot in the crotch to go. For once I'm in and I intend to stay in."

"Lonn has power and he'll use it against us if he wants to. Maybe there's a better way. Lonn said we should make ourselves a pure home. It made me think—we should fix up the trailer court ourselves. That would tickle Dad. And we could get away from Lonn."

"Lonn wasn't talking about this place. He was talking about scumbag people."

"I know, but it made me think of this trashy neighborhood," I told David. "We could clean it up." Why didn't we clean it up ourselves? What were we waiting for, anyway?

"That's the landlord's job." David rubbed the sleep out of his eyes.

"He's never going to fix this place up, no matter how much we complain. Mrs. Kenny said they've been trying for years."

"I'm not cleaning up someone else's crap." David spit the words out. He started putting on his jeans and socks.

"We didn't dump the junk, but it's ours now, because it's in our yard. If we get some guys and a couple trucks, it wouldn't take more than a day. Maybe slap some paint on the trailers. Dig Mom and Mrs. Kenny some flower beds so they can have blooms in the spring."

David didn't respond and shuffled off to the bathroom. I knew it was a good idea. First chance I got I would talk to Dad about it. We could take turns helping each family in the trailer court to do house projects. Get the story in the newspaper. Then I decided I wasn't even going to tell the folks—I'd make it a surprise.

When David and I got to school I was still jazzed about my idea. It filled me with energy in a way I hadn't felt since before we moved to Lodgette. I was standing at my locker when I noticed Eden through the crowd down the hall. I sprinted over, playfully pouncing on her shoulders. She startled and turned around.

"Good morning," I said. "I see you made it to school today without driving off into a field."

"My, my, you're in a good mood." I could tell by her voice that she was still mad about the day before.

"What do you say we go out this weekend? A real date."

She looked surprised. "Are you sure your brother won't be needing you?"

Suddenly I wanted Eden to understand about David. I struggled to find the words. The vision of Trenton's face slid in, but it was all mixed up with David's face. "David's always needed me to help him along," I stammered. "Otherwise he just stands still and lets things run him over." I looked into Eden's face to see if she understood what I was trying to say.

Her voice turned gentle as she answered. "David's sixteen years old, Ben. Are you sure it's not you wanting him to need you?"

I laughed. "He needs me all right. It would have been an ugly sight if I hadn't rescued him from Jason Johnson." Of course I didn't mention what David does to get himself in trouble.

"You seem to be in the hero business," she said. "And speaking of Jason Johnson, I noticed he always says hello to you in the hall. I think he's trying to say he's sorry."

"He's a creep."

"You could get to know him a little before you decide for sure," Eden suggested.

"Eden! The guy knows he can do whatever he wants. He's rich and rotten," I tried to counter. But my idea of a neighborhood fix-up was melting away my frustration and anger. I couldn't help feeling good. I didn't even really feel resentment toward Johnson anymore.

Eden continued her argument. "You've never done anything that was the least little bit mean and then regretted it? I bet you've even done it to David yourself."

It wasn't David but Trenton Biggs I was thinking of and my tongue could not form any more defenses.

"Did Jason get the same punishment as you did for fighting?" Eden asked, even though she knew the answer.

I thought of our day together in detention. "Yeah," I admitted. "He did. You're right. So, will you go out with me?"

"I guess," she said, smiling.

"Friday, then. We'll go to a movie."

"Not Friday." She paused. "It's my brother's birthday. I have to help with the party."

"Saturday," I said. "I'll pick you up around seven."

"You'd better come a little early. I have to introduce any real dates to my mom and dad before they'll let me go."

My hesitation must have shown because Eden laughed. "Don't give me that where-can-I-hide look boys always get on their faces. You won't get parent germs or anything nasty by coming to my house."

On Saturday as I got ready to meet Eden, I saw David sitting at the table glumly pushing food around on his plate.

Mom looked at him and then at me. "Are you going out tonight?"

"I am," I answered.

"What are you boys going to do?"

"I'm taking a girl on a date," I said.

"I see," Mom said. "Maybe she has a friend that can go. Make it a double date."

"I'm not going with them," David grumbled. "That girl is a pain. She's always hopping around like a kangaroo."

I shot him a dirty look. He hardly knew Eden.

"What's her name?" Mom asked.

"Eden," I said, glaring at my brother.

Driving toward Lancy Road, I felt a nervousness in my stomach. But it was a light feeling, not the rock-hard weight I felt every time I thought about Trenton or about my brother sulking back at home.

Eden lived in a new, two-story house with lots of windows. Piles of lumber still lay scattered around in the slush and mud. A cool blue light from the windows reflected on the patches of snow.

Wind blew hard and cold off the nearby river, so by the time I rang the doorbell I was shivering. But whether it was from cold or nerves I couldn't tell. It felt as if my jacket were suddenly too tight, making it hard to breathe.

I started to pick at some wood shavings stuck to my coat from carrying firewood. When I looked up, a young boy was standing in the doorway.

Without speaking to me he yelled in an exaggerated voice, "Hey, Eden, he's here."

"Thanks, bud." I tried to sound playful, as if we were on the same baseball team or something. The boy's face was hidden in the dim light of the doorway.

Eden came to the door, smiling. "Hi, Ben. I see you met my dear younger brother, Greggy the Gruesome, as of yesterday ten years old."

Greg made a face at her and took off running into the house, yelling, "Eden's boyfriend's here."

I felt embarrassed, but Eden took my sleeve and gently pulled me into the house. Her dad was talking on the phone. He was a tall guy and big like a football player. His red-brown hair was a lot like Eden's, only it was pretty shaggy for someone so old.

"That's my dad, Curtis," Eden said. He waved at me but kept talking. Then Eden introduced her mother.

"Hello, Mrs. Taylor," I heard myself saying. My hands felt wet and cold at the same time and I rubbed them on my jeans.

"Call me Toby." Eden's mom was tall like Eden but with smooth blond hair. She was wearing a sleeveless shirt and tight shorts. "I just got off the treadmill," she said. "Have you had dinner? We're going to go ahead and eat. Curtis could be on the phone all night."

I couldn't help comparing Eden's mom to mine: Toby in her sleek exercise clothes and running shoes, my mom in her sweats and slippers. But my mom used to be sort of like Toby. A western cowgirl version. Tight riding jeans, fancy western shirts. *It's going to get better,* I told myself. *Wait till Mom sees the garden beds I'll put in for her.*

"Daddy's making plans to go skiing tomorrow," Eden said, pointing to her father.

"What do you take on your burger, Ben?" Toby asked.

"Just ketchup," I said. I sat down at the dining room table, which was spread with the newspaper and dirty coffee cups. The house smelled of new paint and carpeting. All the furniture was nice, but I could see it wasn't new. Some of it looked really old, antiques.

Eden's mom put a plate with a hamburger in front of me. She cleared away some of the papers as she sat down. Just as I took a bite she said, "So, Ben, do you have brothers and sisters?"

Toby and Eden's brother sat waiting for my answer.

I felt like I was sitting in front of some dating committee or something and the interview had begun to determine my qualifications. I tried to chew my food faster to be able to answer her, but Eden spoke up. "He has a brother, David, just one year younger."

"Where do you live, Ben?" Toby asked.

The food in my mouth turned dry like shredded cardboard. My jaw couldn't push through it. I looked around at the new kitchen and fancy dining room. What could I say? My fix-up plans suddenly seemed stupid and useless. It wouldn't matter to these people in their nice house that I planned to fix up our rotting trailer.

Eden's face looked troubled also. "He lives closer to town, just off

Perry Hill Road." The way she said it, I knew she didn't want her mom to know I lived in a trailer. It almost felt as if the rock I'd thrown through that window was now being flung back at me.

"There are a lot of new houses going in over there," Toby responded. "Eden's dad has been a consultant to several developers. We thought about buying in that area.

"What does your dad do?" Toby plowed ahead. An image of war prisoners being interrogated filled my brain.

Eden tried to save me. "Mom, you're embarrassing the poor guy."

"Oh, go on." Her mother laughed at Eden. "Ben doesn't mind if I'm curious."

Eden whispered, "Sorry about this."

"Did I eat enough for dessert, Mom?" Greg asked.

"Yes, Greg," Toby said. "Do you want cake?" She set a piece in front of me. Not only was I sitting here with the enemy RETCHes, but they were feeding me cake.

"My dad was a ranch foreman over in eastern Montana until last summer," I finally said. I tried to measure Toby's expression to see how far I should go. "But he got fired. He's been unemployed for the last five months." I didn't even mention the job at the Quick Mart. In Toby's mind it might be worse than no job at all.

She looked embarrassed and confused, but then she recovered and went on. "This property used to be a ranch before we bought it and subdivided.

"Benjamin and David," she continued. "Those are nice names. Let's look up the meaning of Benjamin."

"Mom." Eden shook her head. "Not everyone is into that kind of thing."

"Oh, it's fun, Eden," her mom said, laughing. "Greg, go get our name dictionary."

I was actually glad for the change of subject and started to be able to swallow some food.

Toby continued. "We know what your brother David's name means. David was the first king of the Jews."

I tried to control the expression on my face. "David is a Jewish name?"

"So is Benjamin," she said.

I almost laughed. I wondered if my dad had any idea that he and Mom had given both of their sons names from people he hated. But of course he couldn't have. He didn't even know any Jews.

"Here's the book." Greg handed his mom a paperback dictionary.

"Benjamin. A Hebrew name meaning 'son of the right hand,'" Toby read. She smiled, and I could see Eden's smile on her face. "It's a nice strong name."

"It fits you," Eden said. "A hero name."

I wanted to cringe. But I wanted to laugh too.

Just then Eden's dad came in. "I hear you play football."

"I did, sort of," I answered. Eden's parents exchanged looks.

"Well, how did you do this year?"

"Not great," I mumbled.

"Eden told me you moved here from a very small town about the same time we came from Michigan."

"Yeah," I said.

"It can't be easy trying to fit into a big school like Lodgette. Especially in sports, where nobody knows you and you didn't grow up playing with these guys."

He was making me feel better. I heard my voice before I even thought about how to answer. "It was tough. I only got to play a few minutes of each game. Mostly I sat on the bench."

"It takes guts, Ben, to stick with something like that," he responded.

Immediately I thought of David quitting the junior varsity team. Maybe if he had stuck it out, he would have gotten to play more next year. He might have even made the varsity team.

"You should see the cool old truck Ben drives," Greg put in. "A seventy-two Chevy."

"It's just an old work truck," I told Greg.

"I think it's neat," he said.

"Hang on to it," Eden's dad said. "Those older models are easier to fix than the new things."

And suddenly we were gliding into a conversation on engines.

Finally Eden said, "We'd better go. I can see I'm about to lose my date."

Outside, Eden said, "I'm sorry about my folks. They do the question routine to everyone."

"I like them," I told her. And I realized it was true. They weren't exactly the kind of people I was used to. But I did like them.

We sat in the theater and the movie played on the screen, but I didn't see any of it. I couldn't take my eyes off Eden. As I looked at her face in the light from the screen, I became absorbed in watching her watch the film.

"You're supposed to look at the movie," Eden whispered when she noticed me. She leaned close to me. I could smell her warm skin. It was a good smell, kind of like fir needles with something sweet combined. I couldn't stop myself from reaching out and touching her hair.

Eden laughed and smiled at the story in front of her. When she turned slightly toward me I could see the movie reflected in her eyes. She moved her head close as if to whisper something, a small laugh lighting her features. Instead of listening, I kissed her. And she returned it.

In the lobby after the movie we saw Jason Johnson and Jill with a couple other guys from school. They saw us too.

I took Eden's arm and pulled her away from where they were going. "Let's go out the side door," I said.

Back in her driveway I brought the truck to a stop and turned off the engine. We sat silently in the dark until she finally said, "Don't mind those kids like Jason and Jill. You were right about them getting kicks from cutting other people down, but you just can't take it personally."

"I don't mind," I lied. I wanted to move in close to Eden. I wanted to taste her skin again. It seemed as if nothing but being close mattered now.

"My mom and dad thought it was wonderful that you rescued me from the snowdrift." She scooted over on the seat until she was sitting right next to me. Her hand stroked my cheek as if asking a question.

"They're okay," I said truthfully.

I smelled her again and my hands moved around her waist. I saw her lift her mouth to be kissed. Kissing her was like stepping off the edge of a cliff into the clouds.

Eden sat for a moment longer, then whispered, "Good night, Ben." But we had moved beyond the need for words. She got out of the truck. I watched her dark shape rush into the house.

·CHAPTER EIGHT·

Dust

All weekend I thought of nothing but seeing Eden again. On Monday I immediately went toward her locker looking for her. As I came close I saw Jason Johnson standing there with his girlfriend, Jill. They surrounded Eden. No one saw me coming, but I could hear them.

"How could you stand it?" Jill asked Eden.

"She was just using him for his body," Jason answered for Eden.

"What is with you?" Eden asked. "At least Ben Campbell has something different to talk about. He knows a different kind of world. He knows a different kind of Montana life. He's very interesting."

"Cow punching. Fascinating!" Jill sneered.

"Come on," Jason said. "We want to hear all the details. What's it like in the front seat of a truck? Did you have to move the farm tools or are they part of the fun?"

That was all I could stand. Eden was flushed and squirming to get away. I walked up behind them.

"Oh, look. The man himself," Jill said.

"Campbell." Jason sounded surprised that I was there. I even think he turned red in the face, as if he were a little kid caught doing something naughty.

"That's enough, don't you think?" I asked them.

"We were just fooling around, Campbell." Jason leaned against the locker with his arms folded across his chest. "Nothing serious."

Jill was not so light about it. Her smug look contained everything that was wrong with this place and my life. She mumbled under her breath, "So, you're trying to sleep your way out of trailer town."

In the narrow tunnel of my anger all I could see was her face, her smooth cheeks and neatly arranged hair. At that moment I really thought I was going to punch a girl.

Jason stepped in. "Hey, Jill, give these lovers a rest."

Before I even realized he was trying to help me out, I hauled back and slammed my fist into his jaw. And in that one punch all the anger that I'd thought had dissolved spurted through my fist and right into Johnson's face. As my knuckles made contact I realized, *Jason didn't do anything to deserve this.* But it was too late to stop the forward motion of my hand.

"Goddamn it, Campbell," Jason mumbled, and he swung right back at me.

The next thing I knew, Jason was on the floor and I was being hauled off by two teachers.

When I finally became aware of what was going on I heard Eden saying, "Stop it, Ben."

Johnson was sitting up slowly, shaking his head and wiping the blood from his nose.

Jill kneeled down beside him but spoke to me. "You're an animal. Jason didn't do anything."

I looked at Eden but she turned away. Everything drained out of me then, even my breath.

"Both of you." Mr. Grathman, one of the math teachers, motioned to Jason and me. "Come with me." He led the way to Hard-Ass Harrison's office again.

We had to wait in chairs in the office just outside Mr. Harrison's door. The secretary brought Jason a wet cloth for his face. The bell rang, classes started. With nothing to say, we had to sit side by side. I could smell the scent of shampoo on Jason. There were drops of dried blood crusted brown on the perfectly pressed fabric of his pants. I leaned forward, cupping my head in my hands. It was the only place to hide. Sweat had dried to a salty powder in my eyebrows.

Halfway through the period Trenton Biggs came in. I saw his face through the glass of the office door. In an instant I was standing outside his house again seeing the fear in his eyes as my rock went screaming in. But he wasn't looking at me. Trenton was looking at Johnson.

Jason nodded at Trenton. Trenton went to the counter in front of us and waited for the secretary, his back turned to us.

"Do you know him?" I whispered to Jason.

"Of course I do," Jason said right out loud. "I grew up in this town. We were in second and third grades together. Weren't we, Trenton?"

At that Trenton turned around and nodded back at Jason. But all he muttered was a gruff, "Yeah."

"Trenton, this is Ben Campbell." Jason talked on, as if Trenton were dying for conversation instead of trying to avoid us. "I suggest that you, Trenton, stay out of this guy's way. He has a tendency to attack anything that looks even slightly amiss."

"Hey, I'm . . ." I tried to gather my feelings together. "There's been a bunch of tough things going down lately." My voice sounded wilted and torn.

"Man," Jason went on, "I'd hate to be the one to tell you your dog died. Trenton, I suggest you do not mess with the Ben guy."

Trenton had finished his business with the secretary and with one look at me scurried out.

Jason said after he had left, "Trenton's a bit of a lacey boy, but he's all right. Real smart."

"Look, I'm sorry I came down on you." I finally spit out the words. I didn't know why saying sorry was so hard. I *was* sorry. I hated the fact that anger had taken over my brain, if it even was anger. Maybe it was just habit. Which, if true, made me feel even worse. I wanted to feel like I had the day before, when I was mentally planning the neighborhood cleanup. Or even better, how I felt when I was with Eden.

Jason looked at me with a different expression on his face. Finally, after a long silence, he said, "I think maybe I had that punch coming."

Before I could answer him, Mr. Harrison opened his door and beckoned us to come in. He had two folders on his desk that he looked at after sitting down.

"Second fight in just over a month," he said without looking up. "The last time you both served in-school suspension. Obviously sitting you on your rears doesn't send much of a message. I think we sign you up for a month's worth of community service in the afternoons." He leaned back in his chair, folding his hands in front of him and staring at us both.

Jason turned on his polite talking-to-an-authority-figure voice, the one I can never do. "I can explain what happened today, Mr. Harrison."

"I'm not interested," Mr. Harrison answered.

"It's my fault," I said suddenly. "Jason didn't do anything."

Mr. Harrison looked like he didn't believe me or didn't care.

"What kind of community service?" Jason asked.

"I have a friend who is building low-income apartments," Mr. Harrison said. "You will go help the construction crew. It's made up of all volunteers."

"In December?" Jason asked. "In Montana?"

"Yes." Mr. Harrison smiled.

I thought that maybe the smile was from imagining Jason Johnson in his expensive clothes wading through mud and slush.

"When do we start?" I asked.

"Randy Mansfield is the volunteer director for the program. You can report to him tomorrow on North Nineteenth Avenue. Every day, after school, three to six o'clock." Mr. Harrison turned to Jason. "Any questions?"

"I'll be there," he said. It amazed me that even now he sounded full of confidence, as if he were accepting a compliment instead of a punishment. I envied his smoothness.

"Good," Mr. Harrison declared. "Has either of you worked construction before?"

"No," I answered.

Jason shook his head.

"Well, dress warmly," he said. "You may both go back to class now."

As soon as we were outside the office, Jason said, "Thanks, Campbell. That's just what I need. Four weeks of freezing my butt off for a bunch of welfare wimps."

I shrugged. But I could hear in his voice that he really wasn't mad. I couldn't understand it. And the very next sentence surprised me even more.

"You want to ride over to the job together?" he asked me.

I stopped and just stared at him in surprise. I shrugged again. "Why not?"

I hadn't told David any details of my punishment other than that I would be working after school every day for a month. I didn't say anything to my parents. I didn't think they'd really notice since I'd be home by dinnertime anyway.

I was instantly sorry the next afternoon when I met Jason in the parking lot. Two rows over was David standing with Chuck. I think both my brother and I were wearing the same shocked expression on our faces as I got into Jason's car and he got into Chuck's.

Jason saw me staring and shook his head. "You let your brother hang out with that guy?"

"What's wrong with Chuck?" I asked, trying to sound as if I didn't really know who he was.

"He is definitely trouble," Jason answered.

"Look who's talking," I argued. "We're both being sent into hard labor for being just that, trouble."

"Okay," Jason said. "I can be a real bastard. But I know the difference between spoiled-brat bad and total evil. That guy is evil. He hates everybody."

"How do you know?" Standing there looking at Chuck while hearing Jason talk about him, I suddenly found myself thinking about the vandalism, the car, the shooting at the building. I wondered why those incidents felt different from throwing the rocks through Trenton Biggs's window.

"The guy was kicked out of school for breaking into the building and trashing the cafeteria and office four years ago, when he was a sophomore," Jason said. "He has several stints in juvenile detention."

I wasn't surprised. Jason was right. Chuck hated everybody. Lonn hated everybody. Even me. Even David.

·CHAPTER NINE·

Cracks

*R*andy Mansfield met Jason and me at the construction site and immediately put shovels into our hands. For me it was not too different from working on the ranch, and the time went fast. It wasn't so easy for Jason. After about ten minutes he was looking at his watch.

"You have to find a rhythm to the work," I told him. "Then you don't even notice how long you've been at it."

Jason just shook his head. "There is nothing the least bit absorbing about this tool." He held the shovel close in front of him as if he were looking at one for the first time.

It wasn't long before Randy saw that I knew how to work. He moved me to actually putting up boards and asked if I would show Jason everything I did. So I had Jason hand tools up to the roof, where two other guys and I were pounding nails.

Straddling the rafters, I could see far beyond the town to the mountains that rimmed the valley. Each chiseled peak was a different shape and shade in the shadowed afternoon light. Being that far off the ground made me a little dizzy. But I lifted my arms and let my head get light. The town and roads disappeared out of my vision range.

Jason caught me staring off into the distance on his next trip up the ladder. "That triangular mountain is Mt. Blackmore." He pointed south. "Over there is Garnet Peak."

"You know all of them?" I still watched but lowered my arms to grip the solid building frame.

"Jeez, Cowboy." He grinned. "You forget that I grew up here. Hey, do you ski?"

I had to laugh. "At forty bucks a day? Get real." The rich have no idea about money.

"Backcountry." Jason pointed again to Mt. Blackmore. "Hike up, ski down. Doesn't cost a cent. We have a massive collection of skis in the garage that you can use. Want to go Saturday? We'll ask Eden and—"

I cut him off. "Not Jill!"

"Right," he agreed. "We'll just ask Eden to invite someone to go along."

"Maybe," was all I could say. I really didn't know if I wanted to go or not. Jason lived in a different world. A world I didn't understand. He let the subject drop.

The volunteer construction crew was made up of about fifteen people. They all dribbled in, coming from jobs or home. When finished, the project would be three buildings with four apartments in each one. Right now two of the foundations had wooden skeletons standing on them. The volunteers could work only a few hours a day, so progress was slow.

On my second day of working I had watched David once again drive off with Chuck, this time to the regular Wednesday meeting. When Jason and I showed up at the site there was a handful of people already starting. I heard my name called from the group.

"Ben!"

"Aunt Jana!" I was surprised. "What are you doing here?"

"I work every Wednesday after I finish emptying all those bedpans up in the wards." She twirled her hammer as if it were a six-shooter.

"But I could ask what you're doing here," Aunt Jana continued. "Somehow the idea of community work and the name Campbell just don't blend real well."

Despite being a nurse, Aunt Jana knew her way around tools. She and my mom had grown up working on a ranch every summer. Real work, not just in the kitchen. Both sisters could always do as much as a regular full-time ranch worker. When she was younger, Aunt Jana could even rope steers.

"I've been trying to get your mom out here with me," Aunt Jana explained. "But she needs some time."

I agreed but didn't say so. Mom still wasn't herself.

Jason extended his hand to my aunt. "I'm Jason Johnson. Ben's partner in crime."

"We're working here for a month as punishment for fighting in school," I told her straight out, and then added, "I didn't tell the folks."

"I guess I'll have to keep an eye on you, then," she decided. She shook her head. "Since when did you become a fighter, anyway? It sure didn't come from my side of the family."

Before I could figure out how to respond, my aunt Jana and Jason were starting work, side by side. She said to Jason, "I was planning to grill up some burgers when we finish here. Why don't you and Ben stop by?"

"I cannot refuse food," Jason said with a grin. "Ben?"

"Sure." I couldn't get over how easily Jason seemed to be able to talk to people. Sometimes he sounded insincere, like when he was talking to Trenton Biggs, but I was starting to think he really did want to be friendly.

What could people as different as my aunt and Jason Johnson find to talk about? I worked close enough to hear their conversation. Jason was telling Aunt Jana about skiing. Aunt Jana told Jason about one of the other nurses who had been a ski racer when she was our age. Then she talked about some of the more interesting medical cases they had had at the hospital. They must not have known I was listening because I heard Jason start to tell my aunt about the fights we had.

"Man," Jason said, "Ben's got a temper on him. But I gotta admit that both times he was sticking up for the low dog. I was the one being a smart-ass."

When I heard him I felt awful. It wasn't true. I thought of Trenton Biggs, low dog of low dogs. *Blast it,* I yelled in my head. *I didn't hurt Trenton. He doesn't even know me. Forget him.* But I couldn't push those thoughts away.

After dinner with Aunt Jana I was eager to get home. I wanted to find out from David what happened at the meeting. But he wasn't there. Dad said he'd gone somewhere with Chuck and Travis. That didn't settle well in my stomach. I felt like I needed to be with him, looking out for him.

It was late when he came in. I sat up in bed. "Where've you been?"

"Out." I could see the excitement like a sweaty sheen on his face.

"Doing what?" I continued.

He stared at me. "Driving around."

"I know those guys, David. They don't just drive around." As I spoke, my own voice sounded foreign to me. I sounded like some television dad grilling his son.

David must have heard it too. He laughed with a surprised tone of realization in his voice. "You don't like being left behind! Well, now you know how it feels being the one stuck in the crack while everyone just goes on without you."

"What are you talking about?" I asked him.

"Don't you remember that time up in the cliffs behind the ranch when you had those two kids from school over? We were playing raiders and I got my foot wedged in the rock crack. I yelled and yelled for you guys to help me, but you just kept on going."

I remembered. And at the time I had known he was stuck. But in those days David was always crying about something or another. So I had figured he would get over it. "David, that was eight years ago. Besides, you got yourself out."

"Oh, yeah," he sneered. "I got myself out. After yanking on my foot for fifteen minutes. You just ran off and left me. You always left me."

I couldn't believe he was still mad. He was angrier than I could even imagine. He had always been angry and hid it behind the annoying things he did. It was far more than the move to Lodgette; these were deep-rooted feelings.

"I've made some mistakes, David. Not just when you were eight, but recently." I tried to find the words to explain my doubt about what I had done.

"Well, big brother, that is the first honest thing I can remember you saying in a long time." He crossed his arms in a satisfied shrug.

He was enjoying this! The little wimp was almost laughing at me. "Fine," I snapped at David. "But you are in way over your head with those guys. These guys aren't the warriors you think they are. They're just criminals hiding behind a cause."

"That's what the British said about our revolutionary soldiers," David said sarcastically.

I went to sleep trying to understand how I could care about David but at the same time find him so completely annoying.

For the next few weeks I continued to see Eden on weekends. During the week I went to work on the housing project with Jason Johnson. My brother hung out with Chuck and Travis. As we saw less of each other David became more and more tight-mouthed about what they did together.

Just before Christmas break started, Randy Mansfield, the project director, stopped by the job.

"What are your plans for vacation, Ben? Think you'd be interested in putting in some hours?" he asked.

I still had a week of service due him from my punishment, but I realized I wanted to keep working there, Mr. Harrison's orders or not. As I saw the apartments go up board by board I felt as if they were growing inside me too. The higher the walls the fuller I felt. "I'm game," I told him.

"What about you, Johnson?" Randy asked.

Jason looked at me for a minute before he answered. "I was born to ski. But I wouldn't mind coming a couple of days with Cowboy Ben."

"Thanks." And Randy left us to work.

"Maybe we can work out a deal," Jason offered after Randy left. "You've been teaching me to pound nails into wood for long monotonous hours without going crazy, so now I'll teach you to ski."

"Okay," I agreed. I had been getting used to Jason and the idea suddenly sounded kind of adventurous. I liked the fact we'd be hiking up the mountain and finding our own ski trails rather than paying a lot of money at a resort. It was going to be just the two of us, so I could get the hang of skiing before we brought any girls along.

On Saturday morning I left home early, before anyone else was up, and drove over to Jason's house. He lived in one of the new houses on the hill above town. The garage he took me into was twice the size of our whole trailer. It was filled with stuff from tennis rackets to a snowmobile and an all-terrain vehicle. In one corner were what looked like several dozen pairs of skis and a hill of boots.

"Jeez." I stared. "Ever think of opening a sporting goods store?"

"You should see our lake cabin. More boats than family members. Here." Jason threw a pair of what looked like hiking boots at me. "Start trying them on."

At the trailhead below Mt. Blackmore we strapped our skis onto backpacks and started up the hill. The air was thin and cold but once I was warm from hiking it felt wonderful inside my lungs. At the tree line we skirted the edge of a shallow snow bowl and then put on our skis.

"Watch how I do it," Jason instructed. He took off down the hill, cutting graceful slow curves into the untouched snow. It looked easy.

I can do that, I thought as I pushed off. Instantly I felt as if I were flying. The sound of my skis sliding over dry snow was in rhythm with the wind that bit at my face. It was wonderful. Then I tried to turn and found myself rolling in a loose bundle of arms and legs and skis, over and over down the hill. When I finally stopped I was laughing through a mouthful of snow.

"We better start you on some basic snowplow, Campbell," Jason said, pulling me up.

"It's great!" I shouted.

"Just wait until you ski down instead of fall down the hill," Jason said. "Then you'll really have fun."

I don't know how many times we hiked up that hill and skied down, but I do know that once I even went the whole way without falling.

By two o'clock I was exhausted but exhilarated. Heading down the hill, I realized I had enjoyed Jason's company as well as the skiing.

"Would you be interested in helping out with another charity project?" I had decided to share my neighborhood cleanup idea with Jason.

"Maybe." He waited for me to go on.

"The trailer park where I live," I said. "I want to do some real fixing up around there. It's for my mom mostly, but for some others too, like the old lady next door, Mrs. Kenny."

Jason just stared out over the steering wheel without saying anything. I grew embarrassed and felt so stupid for mentioning my idea. *He thinks I'm just a welfare slob.*

When he finally responded his voice was shaky and quiet in an un-Jason-like way. "I'd like to help."

"You would?" I was relieved.

He nodded. "If you think I can." His voice was still unsure. "You've seen me at the housing site. Not exactly a hammer hotshot."

"You've picked up building faster than most guys would," I assured him.

"Really?" Jason grinned. "You know, Campbell, you're the first person who thought I was capable of doing anything besides smarting off."

I doubted that but wasn't going to argue him out of his enthusiasm.

Jason went on. "Won't my father be surprised when I tell him about all my civic services. At least I hope he will. I'd like to see that well-shaven jaw drop for once."

"Wasn't he mad about the fighting?" I asked.

"Me getting in trouble? He's used to that. It's been the same since I was three. Didn't you know I was expelled from an exclusive kindergarten for biting? My dad gave up on me then."

At least all the time I was growing up my dad had been interested in spending time with me. But then I thought about David. Maybe he felt more like Jason did.

Jason drove back to his house, where my truck was parked. "Let's get a group together for the cleanup next Saturday," I suggested as I got out of the car.

"It's a plan," he said.

When I pulled into our driveway, I noticed a large group of cars and pickups parked around the trailers. Coming closer, I recognized both Lonn's truck and Chuck's car. David was loading the pieces of a discarded car engine into the back of Lonn's truck. Teams of people I knew from Guardian meetings were scattered around the trailers, watching over burn barrels or picking up trash.

I went over to my brother. "What's going on?"

Lonn answered. "This is your brother's doing, Ben. He's the leader here."

I turned to search David's face. I tried to ask him the surprised questions that overstuffed my mind. *What is this? The cleanup was my idea. Why didn't you tell me you were going to do this?* But I didn't have the nerve to tell him my thoughts in front of the others.

All David said was, "Now that you're back from the RETCH's house, dig in."

Everyone stopped to watch us, as if they had expected some kind of confrontation. I felt trapped. Keeping my fury hidden was like try-ing to stop myself from vomiting.

Dad started in with his quiet but pressing voice. "It seems as if David's grown to be the leader here. We always thought you'd be the go-getter, Ben."

I thought just how surprised Dad would be at what kind of go-getting David was into at night with some of these same guys who were here playing Dudley Do-right. I almost said so when David tossed me an I-win look that made me just stomp off down the driveway.

·CHAPTER TEN·

Fog

It took me thirty-five minutes to walk the three miles to Eden's. I didn't even realize that was where I was going until I found myself staring at her house. The whole way the frozen gravel on the side of the road scratched under my feet.

I kept thinking about David. *If I had spoken out back there at the trailer court, would things have turned out different? Who did I really care about helping: David, the folks or just me?*

By the time I knocked on Eden's door the sun was setting behind the western hills and the air temperature was falling fast.

Her mother answered the door. "Hello, Ben." She was as friendly as ever.

"Is Eden home? I was wondering if she wanted to walk down to the river with me."

Eden's mother leaned out the door to look at the driveway. "You walked here? Why, you must be freezing. Come in and have some tea or something."

"Actually, I'm warm from walking." But I followed her into the dining room.

Eden was there with her schoolbooks spread out across the table. "Hi, Ben." She looked surprised but happy to see me.

"Would you walk down to the river with me, before it gets dark?"

"Okay, but let's drive up to the bridge and walk the trail there," she said. I could hear the question in her voice. It was as if she could read the unease in my face.

Eden went to get her coat and car keys. "Ben," Toby said as Eden left the room, "can I talk you into staying to eat with us after your walk?"

"I guess," I said. "If it's not any trouble, thanks."

"Then Eden can drive you home later," she said.

As we left, after being in Eden's warm house, I felt the cold sink in. Parking near the bridge, we set out down the path. The only other footprints in the snow were the hoof marks of deer.

We ducked under the ice-weighted branches of hawthorn bushes and around the stalks of last year's wild roses. The gray current pushed its way between crowding ice shelves on either riverbank. Steam swirled above the open water, making a solid fog that could be felt as well as seen.

"It's magical in here." Eden breathed deep. "Like a shining lace veil covering us."

"It does feel like an imaginary world." I tried to memorize how ice and tree melded together in smooth seams. Being there, I had the same feeling of weightlessness as I did sitting on the roof at the construction site or skiing.

"Is something bothering you?" Eden asked. "You seem different today. Quiet, slower."

"It's nothing," I told her, not because I didn't want to talk about my feelings about my brother, but because I just didn't know how to say it.

"Not good enough," Eden said, teasing, but forceful too. "No boy clam-up routine with me. Out with it. Did you and Jason get into it again?"

"No. We skied together today. I had fun." Here I had to fish for words. "That's part of what's wrong, I think. And something happened with my brother."

"With David?"

"Remember the idea I told you about? To do a fix-up on the trailer court we live in?" I watched Eden for signs of embarrassment about where I lived.

But she nodded, so I went on. "I thought I could get some guys together and pick up trash, do some painting. Stuff like that. I even asked Jason if he would help."

"It's a great idea," Eden said, smiling. "I'd like to help too. If Jason can do it, so can I."

"At the time I suggested it, David wasn't interested. But when I came home today I found he had gone behind my back and organized the whole thing as if it were his idea."

"It's good that David took the initiative, even if it was your idea," Eden said. "You should be happy for David. And that he has friends who are the kind of people who do good for the community."

Thinking of Chuck and Travis, I said, "I don't think the cleanup is their idea of community service."

"What do you mean?"

"They prefer to . . ." How could I tell her what we had done? The car burning, the shooting at the building, the rock at Trenton Biggs's house. I could hardly explain this to myself, let alone to Eden. Instead I stopped and put my arms around her. I kissed her, then said honestly, "I'm just mad at David because everybody, including my folks, thinks it was his idea."

"And David let them think that," Eden guessed. She held on to me as if absorbing part of my body. "What did you do?"

"At first I thought it wasn't worth an argument, and I was going to help. But when my dad started grinding in about what a leader David was, I lost it."

"Having seen you lose it before, I can imagine what happened next," Eden said. "You told everyone forcefully that it was your idea." She stepped away from me and we started walking again.

"No, I just left." I broke a piece of ice off a branch. It was so clear I could see the tiny air bubbles trapped inside. Quickly it melted away between my fingers.

"I think you should have stayed and helped even if they did think it was your brother's idea." Eden said.

"I couldn't. I was so angry. I felt as if David was doing it just to make himself look good to our dad and the other guys." As I said this I wasn't sure if I was really angry or jealous. "I was always the one to take the lead on projects. David never was interested in helping with anything. Like working on the housing project with Jason. David always cut it down."

"Ben!" Eden said. "The housing project was a punishment. You had to do it."

We came around the first bend of the river, where the valley widened a bit and we could walk side by side. The reddish rocks on either side of the river were a bright contrast against the clean snow.

"At first it was." I tried to explain how my feelings were changing. "But then I really started to like doing it. And I'm going to keep working there even though I don't have to. I don't think David really cares about having a better place to live or making Mom feel better about the trailer. He did this cleanup intentionally to make me look bad."

"Why would he want to do that?" Eden asked.

Her question sent memories racing through my mind. I remembered all I had taught David to do. I'd taught him to ride his bike and put a worm on a fishhook. But did I also teach him to make himself look good by cutting other people down? I thought about the times that I had let Dad compare me favorably to David. I was a better football player, a better fisherman and a faster runner. So many times I had used David's failures as my rewards. I had pretended to be taking care of him, but often I had only been using him to make me look like the big man. It was no different from what Jason and Jill had done to me at school.

"I think I know why," I told Eden. "And it's my fault."

"Still taking care of him?" Eden asked.

"Maybe now for the first time," I answered. I knew I needed to take action. I needed to make sure David got out of his involvement with Lonn's late-night activities.

Eden suddenly jumped on me piggyback style. "Give me a ride, Ben," she laughed. "I don't want to think about anything sad for a little while."

"Me neither." I wanted to tell her how much better she made me feel. What joy and excitement I experienced with her. But I thought she would laugh. So instead I said, "Miss Eden, if it weren't the dead of winter, I'd set you down and roll you in the grass right here."

"Oh, you think so?" she asked. She leaned over my shoulder and kissed my cheek. "It would be hard to resist you."

Then she slid down to walk beside me again. It was getting late. We would have to pick our way through the dark back to the car. "Your mom invited me to dinner. Think it'll be ready?" I suddenly felt starved.

"If not, we can find a snack to help you through," she said as she patted my stomach.

I took her hand as we walked.

·CHAPTER ELEVEN·

Ice

I went home from Eden's realizing that she was the kind of friend and girlfriend I really wanted. But I needed to be the kind of person in truth that she thought I was. As a start, I would try to save David from making any more mistakes. How could I explain to him what I wasn't even sure of? I was going to try to explain about seeing

Trenton in the shattered window. Then I would describe the feeling of building and of skiing. I had no idea if I could make any sense.

But the minute I walked into the trailer I knew things were different. I no longer had any power over my dad or my brother.

In an angry tone my dad greeted me with, "Where'd you take off to today? Why weren't you here helping your brother? Being a part of this family?"

All of my plans shattered. My tongue couldn't form any ideas that sounded strong and sure.

I couldn't answer him. He continued, "I didn't raise you to run away from helping."

"You did teach us right," I assured him. "It's just that you don't understand everything that's going on. I don't think David should be hanging out with Lonn's guys."

Dad sprang to his feet in a surge of anger. "Lonn is the best thing that ever happened to this family! Don't you start in on the one person who reached out to help us."

I gave up for the time being and ducked into the bedroom. For the rest of the evening I could hear Dad and David, buddy-buddy, cheering at a game on TV. My brother was sitting where I had always been.

Monday afternoon on the job site Jason kept looking at me funny. "What's up, Cowboy?" he finally asked.

Jason Johnson was the last guy I'd ever thought I'd be spilling my guts to. It was just a couple weeks since I had wanted to spill his guts! Without mentioning Lonn or his guys, I told him about my brother stealing my cleanup idea and about my dad's reaction.

He shook his head. "Your brother has a bad case of jealousy. From the way you describe how you and your dad were always tight, it makes me green too."

"You?"

He nodded. "My old man doesn't even notice me unless I'm doing something that embarrasses him, like getting into trouble at school or wrecking his new car."

It's weird how four people can live together in a trailer ten feet wide and forty feet long for weeks without saying what's on their minds, but that's the way our house was. Every day Dad, David and I pretended that nothing was different but everything was. Mom was the only one who tried to get us to talk about the tension that hung in the air. I heard her talking to Aunt Jana on the phone about it. When she saw me coming she whispered to her sister that she would finish telling her later. Between us guys, the unsaid words built up, getting thicker and harder to break.

Every weekday Jason and I put in a couple hours on the housing project. And on weekends I usually did something with Eden. Sometimes we went skiing or snowshoeing; sometimes we went to the movies. If Jason came along, he brought a girl named Ashley with him. We never even mentioned Jill anymore.

What David did I don't know. I suspected he was doing a lot with Chuck and Travis. Many times on weekends he didn't come home. Mom would worry, but Dad always said, "Leave the boy alone. He's finally growing up." Then he would look at me disappointed. It made me feel sick and angry every time he mentioned it.

We kept this up right through January and part of February. Then the weather turned frigid again. Hard wind and snow blew for days, pounding against the trailer.

It was in the middle of a storm one night at dinner that David declared he had a job.

"After school?" Mom asked.

David and Dad exchanged looks across the table. I knew they had already talked this over and the announcement was for Mom's sake only, or maybe for mine.

"No, not after school," David said, his confidence sinking a little, I thought.

"You're quitting?" I asked. I felt every lesson Mom and Dad had ever tried to teach us slide away. Mom and I looked to Dad at the same time, probably with the same expression. He just stared at his plate. Yes, he knew all about it and had already given David his permission. *Hypocrite*, I thought. All these years telling us to study, go to college like he never got to do.

"The boy's going to be working for Lonn down at his garage." Dad's voice was apologetic. "At first he'll just be running errands and such, but Lonn is going to be teaching him the trade."

"Quit school?" My mother sounded weak, almost faint. "Is that right, Frank?"

At that moment I was angry that my mother was not like she used to be. Before we moved she would have exploded and laid down the law about quitting school. But now my mother didn't even question my dad.

"It seems to be the right thing for now. If we were still ranching, it would be different," Dad said. "David's trying to become a man the best way he can."

I sneered at Dad. "Sounds more like they're making a stupid redneck out of David." As soon as I said it I was sorry. The problem was much more complex than calling people names.

"That's enough," Dad shot back. His face turned dark and the muscles up and down his arms contracted. "Your brother is helping this family. We can't make it on the seven bucks an hour I get working at the market or the little your mother has to work so hard for. He's going to bring in a check."

Then I felt guilty again. They did need help paying the bills. I hadn't even thought of it.

David was sitting back, surprisingly calm. In a confident voice he added, "I'll be making money for the family, not for the rich Jew bankers."

"What do you mean by that?" I asked.

"I think you know," he said. He remained like a stone, while my whole insides were trembling in anger and, for some reason, fear. "That welfare housing you work so hard on with the rich guys, who do you think the rent goes to?"

"David's right." Dad sounded so hurt, as if I had punched him. "All that time you spend building houses to make money for the pigs that own this town. And when your brother tries for one day to fix up your own home you won't even help."

"The cleanup was my idea." But it was as if they didn't even hear me.

"I never thought a son of mine would turn his back on us." Dad sat down and started eating. He wouldn't look at me again and I knew that the discussion was over.

But David, the new David, wasn't finished. "I saw there was an article in the paper about that housing project you're working on. It all sounds so good: 'Help your fellow man.' But it's bullshit. It's really about helping the rich pigs get richer, Ben."

"You don't know anything about it," I seethed back at him. But the voice of doubt nibbled at my insides. Would some rich guy benefit from all the work we were doing? Who would collect the rents?

"Lonn knows," David said. "And he doesn't like it."

Then the questions really started bouncing against the inside of my skull like a superball inside the trailer. What did he mean, Lonn knows? And what didn't Lonn like? David pushed back from the table, grabbed his coat and announced, "I gotta go."

Once he was out the door, Mom got going about David quitting school. "I don't think it's a good idea, Frank."

"It's just until we're on our feet again, Donna," Dad insisted. But he sounded as if he was asking for her understanding. "And we need the money. You know that." That ended it. Dad turned on the TV and plunged into his chair. Mom quietly started clearing the dishes.

I followed her. "Why don't you stop him?" I asked.

She stopped midstep and looked at me. "How?"

"Just tell David he can't quit school," I said. "If we were still in Prairie Springs—"

"We're not," Mom said loudly. She sounded more like she used to, almost like Aunt Jana. "It's different here. I'm not sure what is right and wrong now."

I knew Dad could hear us talking, but he didn't say anything.

"But you don't want David to quit and end up working in some cheap motel like you." *Or, worse, being a street thug,* I thought.

"A parent always wants everything for their child, but that's not possible. I wanted both you boys to go to college, but at the same time I wanted you to never leave home. I have to believe you each will find your way."

"I'm not so sure we will," I said, giving up. She didn't want to understand. It was like she and Dad were living in a deep hole and made no effort to climb out.

Later, when I came out of my room to get some water, I surprised my parents. Dad had his arms around Mom's shoulders and he planted a gentle kiss on her temple. He looked embarrassed when he saw me, but Mom's face was at peace.

·CHAPTER TWELVE·

Water

After that night at the dinner table everything changed. I felt my life split out from under my feet like thick ice giving way. David strutted through the days as if he had become more than skin and bone, more than human. And Dad, well, he acted as if his younger son could perform miracles.

"You let David take the truck to his job," Dad told me. "He can drop you off at school."

David spent every day at the shop and hanging out with Chuck and Travis. My brother never talked about what they did, but from occasional articles in the paper I guessed they were the ones who knocked over the gravestones in the Jewish cemetery and spray-painted a church that had hired a black preacher.

Meanwhile, I became dependent on Eden and Jason for rides everywhere. Eden would pick me up in the morning and Jason would take me home after we finished working at the housing project. This went on right into the middle of March.

Eden was too polite to say anything about where we lived being a dump, but I won't ever forget Jason's reaction one day as he stared up the driveway at the group of trailers. "A true tin can." Then he seemed to think about it for a minute and added, "Sorry, Campbell."

"No problem," I said. The words sounded so funny to my own ears. Just four months earlier I would have busted Jason's nose for making the tin can comment, true or not. Now I simply admitted it.

It was the weirdest feeling, like I had become some completely different person but my mind was just now realizing it. I remember seeing a movie once where this white guy gets up one morning and looks in the mirror to find he became black overnight. That's how I felt.

Then one day in the second week of April I found a printed sheet sticking out of the pocket of David's jacket, which was hanging on a nail by the door. I looked over my shoulder to make sure he or Dad wasn't watching and then pulled it out to read.

TAKE ACTION!
Protect your jobs and family from the Jewish threat!

Before I could finish I heard David, out in the kitchen, ask Mom what there was to eat. I quickly stuffed the paper back into his pocket.

Later that day Eden met me at my locker. "Hey, Ben, let's go out to eat lunch today. My treat. I never get to see you during the week, and you and Jason are always working after school." She patted my cheek in the way she had that said she really wasn't complaining.

"Sure." I put my arm around her and started for the parking lot. "I will make up for the neglect of my demanding princess this weekend. I promise."

"Let's pack a picnic and go hike along the river on Saturday. See if we can find some spring." Eden shivered as we walked to her car. The wind was harsh despite the clear sky and sunshine. "I sure wish it would warm up," she added.

"In Montana," I told her, "you can't expect spring until June."

As we drove past the supermarket I spotted David. He was with Chuck and Travis and two other guys. They were placing pieces of neon blue paper under the windshield wiper of each car in the lot.

"There's your brother with those guys you used to hang around with," Eden said, pointing. "What's he doing?"

"I don't know." But as I spoke I recognized the paper as being the same one I had seen in David's pocket.

"It looks like they're distributing a flyer," she commented.

I got nervous. That paper was the last thing I wanted Eden to see. It was bad enough that she knew what a dump I lived in, but if she ever caught wind of what David did . . .

So I tried to shrug the whole scene off. "I don't care what David's doing."

"I think we should stop and see what it is." Eden slowed the car.

"No!" My voice was too loud, even in my ears.

"Okay, okay. No need to get so upset." She sped up again.

"It's just that I know David doesn't want to see me. We hardly even speak anymore."

"I'm sorry, Ben," Eden said. "I wish you and your brother weren't fighting with each other. What happened, anyway? Is it still about the cleanup?"

It was so much more. But what was I supposed to tell her? That I used to dig going around shooting up churches and burning cars? That I turned my brother on to it and now he dug it too? I searched for a safe answer. "We just don't like the same things anymore." It sounded lame. I could tell Eden didn't believe a word I said.

I struggled for a more complete explanation. "David always followed me. It was like he couldn't even think for himself. I played football, so David did. I liked fishing, so David did. But I was always better at everything. Now it's as if he's tired of being second string and is trying to prove he can be better than I am. Plus he needs to rub my nose in the mud at the same time."

"You told me once that you took care of your brother," Eden said carefully, like she was sticking her toe in the river. "Are you sure you didn't do a little nose rubbing yourself?"

I knew it was true. I had known ever since the cleanup. I had taught my brother a lot, including how to be a bully.

On Saturday morning I made plans to meet Eden. Timing was

everything in a situation where she was coming to pick me up. I didn't want to do the introduce-girlfriend-to-parents routine. Dad and Eden shaking hands and chitchatting? Mom and Eden's mom exchanging recipes? I couldn't see it.

The TV was blaring a basketball game when I came out of my room. Mom was bent over, cleaning the oven.

From the green chair I heard Dad's voice shout over the announcer's. "Those bugger basketball players make millions. And for what? Throwing a damned ball around like any kid on the playground." He swiveled in the chair and looked me up and down. "Where are you going?"

I pulled my boots on by the door. "Fishing." I made a point of leaning my fishing pole against the wall. "What time do you have to be at work?" I wanted to be gone before him so he wouldn't see Eden picking me up.

"When I get there," Dad said, pouring another cup of coffee.

I went out the door and walked fast down the driveway to wait for Eden out by the road. Five minutes went by but Eden still hadn't come. I kept looking up to the trailer, afraid I'd see my dad heading for work.

Finally I saw Eden's little blue car coming down the road. At the same time I heard the door of the trailer slamming. Dad was getting into the truck as Eden came to a stop. Before the wheels halted I had the door open and jumped in, trying to squish down in the seat. But it was too late—Dad passed us, staring at Eden and me. The car and truck slid by each other like slow ships.

"Was that your dad?" Eden pointed.

I nodded and watched the truck disappear down the road. I was already thinking what I'd tell Dad when he asked who the girl was. Would he believe it if I said she was just someone from school who happened by and offered me a ride? No way.

"So when are you going to introduce me to your folks?" Eden asked.

I squirmed.

"What's the problem with that, Campbell?" Her eyes were narrowing at me. "It's not as if you're too young to have a girlfriend. Actually, I would think your parents would kind of expect it around now."

"It's not that," I said, still trying to imagine Eden coming for dinner at the trailer. "Things haven't been too good around there lately."

"Is it because my dad makes more money?" Eden glanced sideways at me, as if it would be easier to hear if she wasn't looking straight into my face.

I jumped at the chance to use her explanation. "Yeah, kind of. Ever since my dad lost his job he's been out of sorts. Not what you'd call overly friendly."

"I thought he was working now," Eden said.

"Part time at a convenience store is a long way from being in charge of a huge ranch."

"You're right," Eden agreed. "It must be pretty hard for him."

I felt the point was settled and Eden wouldn't want to come around the family for a while.

When we reached the river Eden parked the car. The snow that still clung to the edges of the bank was dirty and jagged from the rush of water sweeping against it. The wind held the feel of shuddering cold. I zipped my jacket all the way up and Eden pulled a stocking hat down over her ears.

"Let's walk upriver to get warm," Eden suggested. She flung the pack that held sandwiches and a water bottle onto her back.

We walked fast until the river's layered brown banks closed in around us on the trail. When Eden let go of my hand I felt the cold air grip where her warm skin had been. She moved ahead, leaping from one boulder to the next. On the really big ones she scrambled up the side and jumped to the ground from the top. Finally she stopped and waited for me.

"I think I've found our picnic spot." She pointed down.

Behind the rock where Eden stood, sloping up from a quiet side pool, was a place just big enough for the two of us. The sun reflected off the rocks, making a warm pocket between water, sky, stone and ground.

Eden whispered, "Green grass," as she held her hand out to me.

As I stepped into the glade I pulled her into my arms and rested my head on her hair. "I have everything I need right now," I told her. "The sound of the river's voice, the smell of new growth and you." I felt her hug me back.

Finally she broke the spell. "You hungry?"

"Sure." How much poetry is a guy supposed to spout in one lifetime, anyway?

We sat down with our backs against the warm rock. Eden unpacked the sandwiches and a plastic bag of chips, setting them on the ground between us. Suddenly she stopped and looked closely between the blades of grass. Her fingers began to probe, parting the green strands. I leaned over to see what she had found. It was a miniature purple violet. As she touched it softly she said, "Look, spring must be coming after all."

·CHAPTER THIRTEEN·

Darkness

I had some extra money from cutting firewood for Mrs. Kenny, so after leaving the river we drove into town for hamburgers and a movie. It was pretty late by the time we returned to Eden's house.

"Looks like everyone's home," Eden said. Her parents' cars were lined up in front of the garage.

As soon as we came to a stop Eden started to open her door. "Let's go make hot chocolate," she suggested.

"Stay a few minutes." I put my hand on her arm. All evening I had been thinking that I needed to come clean with Eden. She was the one person who would possibly understand the changes I was going through with David, my parents and even Jason Johnson. Maybe she could translate the world and tell me why I had become a foreigner in my own house.

Eden closed the car door. "What do you want to talk about?"

I wanted to spill my guts. I wanted to tell her about burning the car and how I had loved the sense of power. I wanted to explain about throwing the rock through Trenton Biggs's window. I needed to confess that I had dragged my brother into the violence and then left him there to be swept away.

But when I looked into her face the words melted together in my brain like candle wax. I could not make sentences. I took her hand. "It was a great day," I said instead. "I really like being with you."

"I like being with you too," Eden laughed.

Why was it so hard to talk about what I felt, I wondered? "There's more." I forced the words out. "I'm not the same person I was when I met you."

"You sound serious." Now Eden looked puzzled.

"Before we moved here to Lodgette," I tried to explain, "I pretty much thought everyone was just like me and my family. I was popular in school."

"Are you saying that if things were like they were in your old school, you wouldn't be interested in me?" Eden almost sounded angry.

"No!" I said. "That's not what I'm trying to say. Since moving here, things have gotten so mixed up. For a while I didn't understand good and bad anymore or wrong and right."

Eden relaxed and smiled again. She put her hands on my face. "I don't believe there could be anything but strong, steady goodness in you. You saved my life, remember?"

"I'm serious," I said.

Just then Eden's mother opened the door. She called out, "Eden, it's getting late. You'd better take Ben home now."

"I'll just run in and get my heavy jacket," Eden told me, and she slid out of the car.

While she was inside I tried to arrange my thoughts. I was determined to be honest with her. After five minutes and no sign of Eden I began to wonder what was taking so long.

When she finally came back out, she walked slowly, looking at the ground. Her jacket was draped over her arm. Eden got into the car and started it as if she were a zombie.

"What's the matter?" I asked.

She backed out of the driveway without answering.

"What did I say?" Panic came over me. How could she have changed so fast?

"It's this," she said, and she pulled a neon blue sheet of paper from under the folded jacket. She placed the sheet on my leg. I couldn't touch it. I knew what it was.

"My mom said someone put it on her car at the same store where we saw David and your two friends passing out flyers."

I felt hot and cold all over, as if I were burning with fever. Now I unfolded the flyer and finished reading the parts I had not been able to when I found it in David's pocket. There was not a group of people the flyer did not list as enemies. Jews, of course, headed the list, but they were followed by blacks, homosexuals, Asians and people of mixed race. I could hear Lonn's voice, the same one he had used at all the meetings, behind each word. I wondered how that voice, for a short instant, had captured me and lifted me above my unhappiness.

"This is what you meant when you said you used to be different, isn't it?"

"Yes," I told her.

"You were part of this." It wasn't a question.

"Yes. But only at first."

"How *could* you? How could you believe what this says?"

"Lonn makes it sound absolutely real. If you're angry or scared, he tells you why. Like my dad. He lost his job managing a ranch. That's all he knows how to do. Instead of suggesting that he go learn something new, Lonn says, 'It's not your fault.' He says it's the Jews, Mexicans, blacks or homos, whatever group that will make you listen. It was so much easier to just blame someone else for our problems than to solve them."

"Is this why you were so interested in Trenton Biggs?" Eden asked in a quiet voice.

This is it, I thought. *I have to rip open my gut here and let her see me bleed.* "Lonn does more than just hand out flyers and tell guys what they want to hear. He gets guys to go out and do stuff, like throw rocks through Trenton's windows, paint graffiti and worse. I set a Jewish lawyer's car on fire."

"I'm part Jewish." Eden sounded very offended now; her voice level was rising. "You didn't know that, did you? I even have relatives who died in the concentration camps." She grabbed the flyer off my lap and crumpled it up.

"I swear I'm not like that anymore," I said desperately. We were coming close to my house and I knew I had to make her understand. "At first, going out and doing that stuff was like a release. I felt I had some power over my life. But then David started doing it and it was like watching a movie of myself. I didn't like it."

"Do your parents know about this? Did you go to the police? Tell them what this Lonn guy is doing?"

"No, my parents don't know. At least I hope they don't. When I tried to get David to stop he let me know he was just following in his big brother's footsteps."

Eden was silent, a blank silhouette beside me in the dark car. My voice started to sound as if I was begging. "Eden, I can't squeal on my own brother. Even if I just told the police the stuff I did, they'll never get Lonn. He keeps himself clear and safe."

Eden pulled to a stop at the bottom of my driveway. "I don't think we should go out anymore." Her anger didn't crack. She was calm and sure.

"I thought you'd understand," I said.

"I thought you were a hero," she said.

"Out of everybody, I most wanted to be honest with you," I responded, getting angry myself. "I thought you were the one person in the world who would stand up for me and help me."

"Me? This is something only you can fix." Eden looked at me, waiting for my reaction.

I stared at my hands. Every nerve in my body went numb and my throat constricted, causing the tears to build up. "I can't." My voice pushed through the cramped muscles.

"I have to tell my parents what I know about David," Eden said. Her voice was strong. "They won't let me go out with you."

I sat there silently for a minute, trying to think of something that would persuade her to stay. Finally I opened the door and got out into the darkness. The ground and air around me had never felt so bleak before. Eden drove away fast.

Walking up the unlit drive, I went over and over what Eden had said. I knew that when Eden told her parents they would report it to the police. As I approached the trailer I heard the door open. Light from inside framed David in the doorway. He came bounding down the steps but stopped when he saw me.

"It's after ten. Where are you going?" I asked him, but I knew he was going to meet Chuck and Travis.

David grinned. "Business. Big business."

I could see David was excited. I wondered if I should tell David that Eden's parents might be calling the police as we spoke. After all, it was my fault that David had gotten into this. "Don't do it, David," I said. "It's wrong."

"Wrong? I'm doing what's right. I'm cleaning up your messes, brother."

Right then I knew what they were planning. The housing project. They were going to hit on my work. I chose my words carefully. "The police are going to know you were passing out those hate flyers."

"How could they know that?" he asked.

I hesitated, then said, "Someone from school recognized you. I heard them talk about it."

"It's that girlfriend of yours, isn't it?" David glared at me. Then he became smug. "It doesn't matter. There's no law against passing out flyers. Free speech, remember?"

"Don't be stupid, David. It's not going to take the police long to put things together. They'll figure out you're connected with the graffiti and the mess at the cemetery. If you do something more tonight, they'll be on you faster than a crazy bull."

"They'll be after you too," David said, still smug. He pointed a finger at my chest. "Or have you forgotten your little fun with the gun?"

"I know," I whispered. Behind us a car pulled into the driveway. I recognized it as Chuck's.

"It's time to do battle," David announced.

"Don't," I pleaded. "Stay here." In that second I realized that even though I had never done right by my brother, I really loved him.

"You don't get it, do you?" David taunted. He moved in close to my face so that his anger rolled over my skin with his breath. "I like it! I like the feeling I get when I show the kikes and the niggers and the mudskins that I'm stronger than they are." He turned and walked straight and swiftly to the waiting car.

"The cops will be on your ass tonight," I yelled. It was as useless as trying to catch snow in the palm of your hand.

I sank down onto the wet, cold ground and felt the dampness seep into my jeans. My head fell into my hands and I knew I was crying, sobbing as if I were a little kid again. In the last thirty minutes I had lost the two people I cared about most. No matter how cold I got, I couldn't move. It was difficult to suck enough air into my lungs.

Time was measured only in moonlight. After what felt like seconds and weeks all at the same time I raised my head. The cottonwood trees had tiny new sprouted leaves that quivered in the silver light.

I stood up shaky and numb. I got myself into the trailer, talking to keep myself focused. "Keys, where are the keys?" I tried to move quietly so I wouldn't wake my folks. As I rummaged through a junk drawer I heard a noise.

"I heard what you said to David," Mom said from where she stood in the bedroom doorway. Tears ran down her cheeks, leaving wet trails that picked up the light from the kitchen.

"I'll stop him, Mom. I promise."

"Where is he going?" she asked, starting to move in her strong way, as if we were launching a search for lost calves on the range. She gave me hope.

"North Nineteenth. The housing project." I found the keys and headed for the door.

"I'm phoning the police," she said.

Hesitating, I said, "Dad might not want you to."

She looked shocked. "Of course he will, Ben."

I hurried and started the truck while coasting down the driveway. I knew Chuck and David must be headed for the housing project. What were they planning on doing there?

As the construction site came into view, I slammed on the brakes.

"Oh, God, no!" I cried out loud. Flames were starting to rise at the base of the half-finished buildings.

·CHAPTER FOURTEEN·

Fire

The growing flames loomed ahead as I pushed on the gas pedal. I didn't slam on the brakes until the truck hit the sidewalk. And I was out and running across the muddy ground almost before the truck stopped completely. As I got closer I could see that it wasn't the actual building on fire, but a pile of scrap wood set close against the building so that the fire would look like an accident.

I kicked at the wood to scatter the burning pieces away from the walls. As soon as the building was safe my panic settled and I had to rest my hands on my knees. I took deep breaths and tried to calm my trembling.

I heard voices from behind the building. David, Chuck and Travis along with two guys I didn't know came into sight, laying small bundles of hay every few feet along the base of the building.

Chuck was the first to notice that the starter fire had been snuffed. He looked around in the dim light. He saw me and yelled to David. "Damn it, Campbell. Get rid of your brother."

David ran over to me but I stopped him. "I'm not going to let you do it!" I yelled.

I reached out for my brother's shoulder, but he twitched away from me. "I'm sick of you bossing me around," David said. "I'm making my own decisions now. I'm defending you."

"Me?" I yelled again. "How are you doing that?"

"I'm destroying this project you've been working on to save you from getting sucked into the Jew conspiracy! A RETCH project, Ben. You remember the RETCHes? It was you who explained it to me. Now you've become one of their slaves, and I'm here to free you."

"Come on, David!" Chuck shouted to him as he squirted lighter fluid over the bundles. "It's time."

Chuck, Travis and the other two started to light the saturated piles of straw. I saw the blaze being born and ran for them, pushing my brother out of the way. I tore off my jacket and hit the flames with it. The fire still spread until my coat caught fire in my hands and I had to drop it as the heat seared my arms.

From behind, David grabbed me and pulled me down into the mud. I swung my arm and hit David in the side of the face. At the same time I felt David's fist slam hard along my cheekbone. The pain made me dizzy and sick to my stomach. I heard myself groan as I tried to roll away. I could taste the vomit in my mouth.

David kept hitting me even when I curled into a ball. My brother, who had always retreated at the first sign of blows, had become a fighting fanatic. Another lesson I must have taught him. As I tried to keep from passing out I could see the flames begin to feed themselves on the walls of the building.

Then I heard the sirens. I felt David stop as he looked down the street to where the sound was coming from. "You stupid, stupid . . . ," David hissed.

I was about to tell David that his own mother had called the cops, but he took a step toward running away. At that instant my anger overtook my pain. All I could think of was that I wanted David to be caught. I reached, intertwined my fingers around his leg and held tight. David fell like a heavy tree. His breath shot out of him as he struck the ground.

I then flung myself over David to keep him down. From the blackness beyond the flames I could hear Chuck and the others yelling, "Come on. Let's get out of here."

David also heard them and struggled under me. Even though my lip was split I chanted to myself, "Just hold him." Finally I saw the flashing lights gather around us.

Then I felt arms everywhere. Four lifting me off my brother and pulling me away from the burning building. I looked around to see two policemen holding David and other cops leading Travis, Chuck and the others to the ring of police cars.

The police were asking me questions but I couldn't hear. My ears burst with the sound of fire sirens pulling up to the scene. I still thought I was going to be sick and I stumbled. The police tightened their grip on my arms.

"We need a medic over here," I heard one shout.

It's strange, but it wasn't until they started to look at the burns on my arms that I was aware of any pain. When they pointed out the burns I started yelling. The paramedics immediately loaded me into an ambulance.

At the hospital, the doctor cleaned and bandaged the burns on my arms. He also gave me something for the pain. It didn't take long before the medication made everything feel slow and fuzzy.

When they were finished cleaning me up and making sure nothing was broken, I was handed over to the police. A man and a woman sat me down at a table in one of the hospital conference rooms.

"I'm Detective Harper," the woman said. "And this is Detective O'Neill. You need to tell us what happened tonight."

I tried to make my brain function through the pleasant blanket of pain medicine. I slowly told them the whole story, beginning with moving to Lodgette. I was honest about what I had done with Chuck and Travis. Then I tried to explain how my feelings had changed. Telling the whole story felt like the end of winter. It felt like I was starting over new.

"Can you tell us about Lonn Monroe's involvement in the vandalism and violent acts?" Detective Harper asked.

"Lonn Monroe?" My mind couldn't focus for a moment. I didn't think I had ever heard Lonn's last name.

"Lonn Monroe," Detective O'Neill repeated. "Did he tell you to shoot into the synagogue? To set the car on fire? Did he plan it?"

"I think so, but it was Chuck who always explained the details of what we were going to do."

"But Monroe knew about the incidents," Detective Harper stated.

"Yes," I answered.

The two detectives then spoke in whispers together and wrote notes for several minutes before turning back to me.

"We believe what you've told us," Detective Harper said. "Two of the other suspects couldn't identify you tonight."

I remembered the two new guys.

"You will be expected to answer charges connected with the damage to the synagogue and the Second Street office building." Detective Harper told me. "You'll appear before the juvenile detention officer a week from Wednesday, nine A.M." She handed me a paper with the time and address written on it.

"What about my brother, David?"

"He's in custody," Detective O'Neill said. That's all they would say.

Gathering up their files, they left, saying, "You can call your parents to come pick you up."

A nurse brought me a phone. I dialed the number.

"Ben, where are you?" Mom's voice was frightened.

I heard myself speaking as if from a great distance. "I'm at the hospital. I'm all right. Can you come get me?"

"Where's David?" she asked.

"He's in jail," I said.

I could hear my mom turn away from the phone and tell Dad

what I had said. There was a full silence in the background.

But then very quietly Mom said, "Wait there. I'm going to drop your dad at the jail first, then I'll come for you."

I sat in the waiting room for an hour, letting the medicine melt my insides. The nurses kept staring at me. Twice they asked when my parents would come for me. I couldn't stand people looking at me any longer, so when the nurse at the counter was busy on the phone I quietly and quickly walked out the door.

From the hospital I walked back toward the housing project. The fire was out when I got there. A few firemen were cleaning up. It was still a bit dark and I strained to guess how much damage had been done. Even from where I stood across the street I could see that the walls were intact. I hoped we could repair any damage.

Our truck was no longer parked where I had left it. I figured my parents had picked it up. As I stood there, one of the firemen noticed me, so I walked away.

·CHAPTER FIFTEEN·

Daybreak

The sun rose as I walked around, repeating in my mind everything that had happened in that strange night. I started with Eden telling me she wouldn't see me anymore, the fire, David's arrest and then my folks not coming for me at the hospital. I think I was in shock, kind of, because I felt totally empty. It was like I had died and left the world behind. Now there was only a shallow spirit left, released to wander some blurry unknown land.

I roamed ghostlike around the neighborhoods, watching the lights come on in houses. I smelled wood smoke from one house and it made me shiver in the spring cold. I could picture the people inside starting their day, getting ready for work or school.

All these people still have a life they can touch, I thought, *like the solid walls of their houses.*

It was more than an hour before I ended up on the street where my aunt Jana lived. The truck I had left at the housing project was parked in front. As I came closer I heard arguing from inside.

Stopping to listen, I recognized my mother's voice. "He didn't know, Jana. Neither of us did."

"That's hard to believe," Aunt Jana said. "Frank had to have known. How could he have gone to all those meetings and not gotten some idea?"

"He blames himself," Mom said, defending Dad. "When I told him what was happening he was crushed. He said all he thought about was how Lonn got him a job."

In the pause I knocked on the door. When it swung open Aunt Jana exclaimed, "Where did you come from? Look at your face!"

I felt the side of my cheek where David had hit me. It was tender and I knew there must be a bruise.

My mom rushed to me and hugged me. "When I got to the hospital you'd taken off. I've been so worried, Ben."

Then Aunt Jana noticed the bandages on my arms. "My God! Come inside." Both sisters led me to a chair. I noticed Aunt Jana was in her nurse uniform and had a bowl of cereal half eaten on the table.

It was already past seven. "I have to be at work by eight," she said.

I took the mug of coffee she set in front of me. As I grasped the cup my arms throbbed and I felt exhausted.

"Where's Dad?" I asked.

"He's still at the jail," Mom answered.

"Tell us how this could happen," Aunt Jana pleaded. "How did your father get you in with these awful people?"

I looked to Mom, trying to read her face.

"He didn't know," I said. Mom's relief was obvious. "Maybe he should have known," I told them both. "But Lonn is very careful to keep what his guys are doing hidden. At the meeting there are always new people he doesn't know, people who come once and don't return, so he doesn't mention the violence. I'm the one who is to blame. I got David into this stuff." I told them everything that had happened.

When I was finished Mom said, "I didn't see it. None of it."

"Don't blame yourself, Donna." Aunt Jana took her hand across the table. "This has been a hard time. You've been wrapped up in just trying to survive."

"No." Mom shook her head. "Our life from the very beginning has been wrong. It must have been." She spoke in statements but looked into my face for answers. "Our life taught you to hate people you didn't even know. Our life taught you to blame other people for your problems. I am responsible for that life."

She began to sob. Aunt Jana said, "What about Frank? Why hasn't he said something to these boys that will help them?"

"We're all to blame," Mom said.

Aunt Jana had to agree. "We didn't come from families that were very good about talking things through."

I felt exhaustion sweep over me.

"You'd better go crash on the couch," Aunt Jana said.

She gathered blankets and a pillow and made me a bed on the sofa. "Come get some rest." She gently tucked the covers up around my shoulders. I was glad I was there.

Mom came and sat on the edge of the couch. "How do you feel?"

"I hurt," I told her. "But I think I can sleep."

"I'm not surprised," Aunt Jana said. "Now, I have to get to work."

"As soon as Ben feels rested we'll head home." My mom's voice sounded as tired as I felt.

"Let me help in any way I can," Aunt Jana told Mom.

At ten o'clock on Monday I sat with Mom and Dad in the back of the county court. Aunt Jana came in and slid in beside us.

"Anything new?" she asked.

Mom and Dad both shook their heads.

"I tried phoning Lonn's shop," Dad told her. "But whoever answered just hung up on me."

"I'm glad you tried," Aunt Jana told him.

Dad looked surprised to hear a compliment from Aunt Jana, but he nodded and accepted it.

Near the front, I saw several people I recognized from Lonn's meeting. Lonn wasn't there.

But what surprised me more than Lonn not being there was that Eden was. She sat with her father in the middle of the courtroom. I couldn't stop myself from staring at the back of Eden's head. And as if she could feel my eyes like a breeze, she turned around. Her face was unreadable.

Soon they brought in David, Chuck, Travis and the others, seating them in the front row. Everyone stood as the judge entered.

The hearing didn't take long. My brother and the other guys were each appointed a lawyer. The prosecutors asked the judge to schedule the arraignment for a future date so they could have time to prepare. They called it a hate crime and this seemed to make the charges more serious.

I whispered to Aunt Jana, "What do they do at the arraignment?"

"That's when David will enter a plea of guilty or not guilty and they'll set a date for the trial," she said.

The prosecutor told the judge they wanted to charge the defendants as adults. I cringed. I knew that if David was found guilty, he would go to the state prison. That's when Mom broke down crying.

I wanted to stand up and yell, *This is my fault. I got my brother into this. I should be the one you send to jail.* But I also wanted my parents to tell me everything was okay. That David wouldn't go to jail. That I wasn't responsible.

Bail was set for each of the four. They were then led away and the hearing was over. In the hall outside the courtroom Mom hugged me while Dad stood back with his hands stuffed into his pants pockets. Finally, still looking at the floor, he said, "I'm sorry, Ben." I could see how much he was trying to say with those words.

Then, as if I were the parent and he were the child, I put my arms around him. He held me tight.

Finally Dad dropped his arms, took my mom by the hand and said, "Let's go, Donna."

"Are you coming, Ben?" Mom asked.

"In a while," I answered as I nodded toward where Eden and her father were standing.

After my parents were gone I sat back down heavily onto the bench. I felt someone sit down close to me. Thinking it was Aunt Jana, I didn't look up. But then I heard Eden's voice. "I saw how hurt your parents are. I'm so sorry for you all, Ben."

Blindly I reached for Eden's hand. Clasping her warmth like a prayer, I held it to my lowered forehead. She felt so comfortable next to me that no more words were needed.

But out of the corner of my eye I saw her dad watching us. *He must hate me more than Eden does,* I thought. He came over to her. "I'll wait for you in the car."

Eden and I sat for a few minutes more.

"I can't stay," Eden whispered.

"I'm sorry," I struggled to say.

"You did the right thing, Hero." Her kindness hurt.

I tried to say, *Maybe we could start over.* Maybe now I could be better at telling her what was going on inside me. But no words came out.

"I've got to go," she said.

·CHAPTER SIXTEEN·

Bone

In the days after David's hearing, my parents tried to act as if everything were okay. But I heard them up late in the night talking quietly in their bedroom. Mom forced herself to shed her quiet withdrawal and began to at least sound like she used to. She made my dad promise to quit the job at the Quick Mart as soon as he found something different. He was relieved, and her energy seemed to give him hope.

On Wednesday Mom came into my room. "Ben, get up. Go back to school. You stayed in bed all day yesterday. That's enough."

I didn't move. All I could think about was having to face all those students and teachers staring at me.

"I'll give you a ride on my way to work," Mom said.

"I can't do it, Mom. I can't go out there yet. Everyone knows what happened. They'll all be talking about me."

"Yes, they will," she agreed. "Just like the women at the motel will be talking about me. But we have been avoiding our problems for way too long in this family. It has to stop. I'll write the school a note saying you've been absent because of family problems."

I groaned. Then I sat for a minute trying to summon the will to go on.

Later, as I got out of our truck in front of the school, I saw a group of kids staring at me. Passing by, I heard one of them hiss, "Nazi." I walked on as fast as I could.

Inside the door I stopped to get myself together. How many other people there knew what had happened over the weekend? The story had been in the paper the day before. My name hadn't been mentioned specifically in the article, but Lodgette was a pretty small town; news got around fast.

I felt my teeth clatter with nervousness as I walked through the door. In the office I handed the note my mom wrote to the secretary. When she took it briskly from my hand, I wondered, *Does she know?* Was she reacting angrily to me or was she just in a hurry?

As I went down the hall I felt people must be staring at me. And even though I mostly watched the floor, I could almost feel them pointing me out and whispering. Then I saw Eden. When she saw me, she stopped and looked unsure for what felt like forever. I was torn as to whether I should rush over to her and throw myself into her arms or run the opposite way. Finally another girl spoke to her and Eden walked away in the direction of her class.

After Eden was gone my whole body began to tremble and my lungs felt as if they were collapsing. I knew I wasn't going to make it through the day. I ducked into the art room.

I closed the door behind me, leaving the dusty smell of the hallways for the strong scent of turpentine and ink. It was quiet and empty. But then someone came out of the storeroom.

"Ben!" The voice sounded surprised. "You don't look so good."

"Jason? What are you doing here?"

He shrugged with a half grin. "I like to mess around in here—Woodcuts, mostly. My old man says that art will never support me. He doesn't let me take the classes. So I do it in the mornings and during study hall."

"I didn't know that," I said.

"I'm not very good. I don't really advertise the fact. Anyway, Ben, how are you?"

"Eden won't even talk to me," I murmured.

Jason sat down across from me. "I gotta say, Cowboy, I knew you had a temper, but you don't seem like the skinhead type to me. You even got to like me and that can't be easy."

"I thought I was one of them," I said. "I tried to hate everyone and blame them for what was wrong in my life, including you."

"What happened?" Jason asked.

"When my brother got in on the action—you know, the crime stuff—it was like watching myself."

"You hate yourself," Jason repeated. "So what makes you different from a lot of other people? Come on in and join the club."

I looked at him, amazed. "Oh, right. You're telling me that you hate yourself. Rich RETCH with the big house, big car, big checking account." It made me mad that Jason could think he had experienced anything like I had.

"RETCH?" he asked.

I felt embarrassed as I explained. "It stands for 'rich enough to cheat.'"

Jason looked me straight in the face. "Daddy's house, Daddy's car, Daddy's bucks. My whole life he has made it clear that I didn't deserve any of it and that if he didn't take care of me, I'd end up as trailer trash. Sorry, Ben. His words, not mine."

I still couldn't buy the poor-little-rich-boy line, but Jason seemed at this moment the only friend I had. "I'm not only trailer trash but a criminal as well. So how do I get out?"

"Start over?" Jason suggested.

"How?"

"You're asking the person my father calls the stupidest child ever born." Jason tried to make a joke but I didn't think it was funny. He became more serious. "You taught me, Ben, when we were building the housing project. You start at the bottom and work up, one nail at a time. Remember how you told me to find a rhythm to the work?"

"Yeah," I answered.

"You were right," he said. "I think maybe this is the same. Each step you take will make the next one visible."

I didn't really understand him but I said, "Thanks, Jason."

He nodded. "I'm pretty glad we crashed into each other, Campbell. Anytime you want to hang out, you know, pound some nails, shovel gravel . . ." He left the sentence unfinished, smothered in a laugh.

Jason's advice felt good, good enough to go on.

For the rest of the day I shuffled through classes almost unaware of anything that went on around me. I stopped noticing if there were stares and gestures. I didn't hear what teachers said or what lessons were done. But a plan grew deep inside me.

As I walked into the trailer that afternoon I saw my dad was on the phone. "You tell that bastard Lonn he better talk to me."

There was silence as he listened to the response, and I stood in the doorway looking at him. He was crouched in angry tension over the phone as if he might punch the person he was talking to right through the line.

When it was Dad's turn to speak again, suddenly his whole body changed expression. He stood up straight and answered in a quiet voice, "I will see Lonn in court, then. And all that needs to be said will be."

Dad hung up.

"It's the best way, Frank," Mom told him. "What can you say to him over the phone? He won't listen."

"It would make me feel better," Dad said to both of us.

"To Lonn, David and guys like us are just the expendable dummies in the trench," I said. "If we get blown away, he can always find new foot soldiers. He simply steps over the bodies and goes on."

"Well?" Mom asked me then. "You survived the return to school?"

I told Mom and Dad about my conversation with Jason. Then I described how Eden had avoided me. This was something brand-new that Mom said she was going to make Dad and me do. Forced communication, she called it. Every day we would have to sit down and talk about everything we'd done that day.

"But I'm not going to let this thing with Eden end in silence," I said. "I'm going to call Eden until she lets me see her."

It wasn't as easy to pull off, though. When I phoned her house no one answered. I left a short message and decided to try again later.

But no one ever answered. She never returned my calls. And at school it was as if she had disappeared. The girl who had drifted into my life with the snow now melted away.

·CHAPTER SEVENTEEN·

Skin

*O*n Saturday morning when I woke up the sun was already coming through the small windows. It made a puddle of golden light on my floor. The luxury of *not* having to go out where people would stare at me was a relief.

All through this difficult week the only good thing was Jason.

After we'd talked in the art room he had spent the rest of the week sticking up for me. I was glad I'd bloodied his nose, even though it's a strange way to make a friend.

I smelled coffee and heard Mom moving around in the kitchen.

"So," she said when I came through the door. "Your dad is already up and out looking for a new job."

"Do you think he's going to be all right?" I asked.

"He has to be. We have to be, all of us," Mom said. "What about you? What are you going to do?"

I pushed the hair out of my eyes. "Start looking for an after-school job," I said. "Then when I have my hearing I'll be able to say I'm trying to do something okay with my life. I'm going to talk to Randy Mansfield about working for him."

"You should also look at the want ads." Mom took the section out of the paper and passed it to me.

I poured a cup of coffee and sat down to look through the list. "Here's one. Part time at the burger place on Main Street."

"Sounds fine," she said, joining me at the kitchen table.

"I'm also going to work on fixing up our trailer and the neighborhood."

"Whether David's reasons were good or bad," Mom said, "he did manage to get the garbage cleared out."

I tried to swallow my bitter feelings about David's project. "How about starting with a coat of paint on the trailer and a white picket fence in front of the place?" I offered. "Then I'll dig you flower beds and some for Mrs. Kenny."

"Oh, Ben. That would be wonderful. I think I'll go by the plant nursery after I get off work."

I folded up the paper and watched her leave. I didn't really know if everything was ever going to be all right. But that day I would just shoot for a little serenity.

After Mom left I went outside and started the lawn mower. I cut the shaggy grass in front of our trailer and Mrs. Kenny's. Then I drove stakes with string tied to them, lining out where the fence would go. As I finished, my aunt's car pulled up. Aunt Jana climbed out.

"How are you, Ben? Do your arms hurt?"

I shook my head. I had taken off the bigger white bandages the day before, leaving only a few Band-Aids.

"Mom went to work," I told her.

"I figured she had," she replied. "I was hoping to see you."

"About what?"

"I wanted to tell you that I think you have a lot of courage. It was you who faced up to the truth of what that con man of a preacher was doing to you and your family. It was you who walked away."

"I didn't walk away, Aunt Jana," I said, trying to be honest. "I tried to sneak out the back door. I tried to get away without saying what I knew to be true and saving David and Dad from a lot of pain."

"At first, perhaps, but I can see by the way you stand and look and hold your head that you will never sneak away from anything in the future. You will save more than just your family."

Aunt Jana's confidence in me made me feel stronger and more sure of myself.

"What's the news about David?" she asked.

"Mom and Dad are meeting with the lawyers again this week."

"And that preacher? What's going to happen to him?"

"The police haven't been able to find Lonn."

"I'm not surprised," Aunt Jana said.

"I told Dad that Lonn's lying low, hiding out until the pressure is off. Maybe even getting ready to move and start over someplace new."

"I don't think anything serious is going to happen to this guy because of what he got you boys to do," Aunt Jana said.

"Dad was really hurt when he realized Lonn was using him and us. He's out job hunting right now."

"I'm happy for your mom's sake. It shows he's got some gumption after all."

"Wow," I teased. "You said that about Dad?"

"Will you mention to your mom that I came by? I want her to know I'm here for her," Aunt Jana said.

"She'll be glad you came," I said.

In the afternoon I drove into town to talk to Randy Mansfield about a job. He answered the door when I knocked. From the look on his face I could tell he knew all about the trouble with Lonn, so I just plunged in. "Everything that happened," I stammered, "I'm really sorry for it."

"I'm glad to hear you say that," he said.

I did hear honest relief in his voice. And he looked as if he wanted to hear my explanation. "I want to make up for what I've done, the trouble I caused in town. But I need to work. For money, that is."

He looked like he understood. "I might be able to help in a month or so, when the summer building season gets going. Come talk to me then."

"Thanks," I said. Then I hesitated, trying to word the question that still clung to me. "The housing project. It *is* nonprofit, right?"

Randy looked confused. "Yes. Rents are subsidized to make them affordable and all the materials are donated or bought at cost. No one's getting rich here."

"Thanks, Randy," I said. "I'll still be working on that project whenever I can."

"I'll know where to find you, then, when I can offer a paying job, Ben."

Next I filled out job applications with Barry's Burgers and Wilson's Yard Maintenance. After that I headed straight for the river.

The wind was cool but the sun was warm. I rolled down the window and let the new air wash over me. That's the way the seasons change in Montana, from frigid to sweltering in thirty seconds flat. I pulled my cap down over my forehead so I could see the road without the sun glaring in my eyes. On the straightaway I hit seventy. As the truck sped up I could feel the guilt and anger steam off my body like old skin peeling away.

Along the river I parked the truck and, taking a water bottle, headed upstream. I followed the same trail Eden and I had used just a month earlier, when she found the spring violets. Now green grass was sprinkled with yellow glacier lilies and I could see the small stalks of other plants poking up through the damp earth.

The river water was gray with melting snow and it ran heavy. It covered some of the rocks where Eden had climbed and jumped. The image of her on that day was almost real in my mind.

Around the next corner was our picnic spot. As I approached I could see the feet of a person sitting near the rock. A brown paper bag was set nearby. Someone else had discovered our place, so I would have to find another. Keeping my eyes on the water as it skimmed past, I walked on.

"Ben?" I heard a surprised voice. I knew that sound so well. But still it made me jump.

"Eden? What are you doing here?"

"What are *you* doing here?" she returned.

I was flustered and shifted my water bottle from hand to hand, trying to think of an answer that was believable. "Why didn't you call me back? I've been needing to talk to you."

"I couldn't think of what to say. I didn't know what my feelings were," she said.

To me she seemed whole, the way I used to feel in my old life. What could I say to her? She had every right to want me gone.

"Don't go," she told me, as if she knew my thoughts.

I stepped closer to her.

"I've come here several times," Eden admitted.

There was a sudden wondering in her voice that I could hear. It made a quiver start to grow deep inside me.

"Will you sit for a while?" she invited.

I lowered myself into the grass cross-legged. As I did she reached out and moved a stray bit of hair off my forehead. I couldn't tell what she meant by this touch. Was it just the expression of an old and sorry friend? What I really wanted to do was to kiss her. Kiss her hard and long. I wanted to hold her next to me as if she were glued on. Instead, I started nervously picking at the sole of my shoe.

After sitting there in the uncomfortable silence Eden finally said, "Why didn't you talk to me about this? If you had only explained what was going on . . ."

"Sure, tell you my brother and I got our kicks by harassing homosexuals and shooting up churches."

"You don't think I could have understood what you were struggling with?"

I knew now was the time to try to really open up with her. But still, saying these things didn't come easily. "I didn't understand myself. I wanted to tell you sooner. I wish I had." I hated how shaky my voice sounded.

"Me too," Eden said. "It hurt me that you weren't up-front with me."

The sound and smell of the water pressed against me. Small breezes rose off the moving river. I tried to let its movement ease my thoughts.

"What are you going to do now?" Eden asked.

"Pound one nail at a time," I answered.

She looked confused, so I explained. "You know, one step at a time. Stay with my folks and help them as much as I can. Go to school. Get a job. Try to find ways to mend what I've broken."

"What about college?" Eden introduced a subject I hadn't even thought about.

"I don't know," I said.

"If you want something—" Eden started.

"That's easy for you to say," I interrupted. "Just like your driving. You plow straight through the drifts to wherever you want to go. If you get stuck, someone is there to help you."

"I guess it is easier for me in a lot of ways," Eden said. "But I don't think you should be afraid of dreaming."

I thought how cloudy my future seemed. It was hard to think past the next week, let alone the next year. I needed to stick with Jason's advice: one step at a time.

Eden ran her hand over the grass thoughtfully. "I keep remembering the way you looked the day you rescued me on Mason Road. I had never seen anyone so confident and capable. You knew what the right thing to do was and you glowed with that feeling. That's the real Ben, the hero. But somewhere you lost him."

"I did," I admitted.

Eden got to her knees, so her face was even with mine.

I reached out my hand and cupped the back of her head, drawing her close. I kissed her, knowing every hopeful word she said was a gift.

When we parted she sighed and looked at the rocky hills beyond the river. "I'm not ready for this, Ben. I'm not sure."

"Sure of what?" I asked, but I knew what her answer was going to be.

"You."

I remembered the first time I had ever kissed Eden, in the movie theater. Ever since then I knew she was somehow part of what felt right. "I'll never stop proving myself to you," I said.

Eden took my hand, smiling at me with all the warmth of hope. I felt what she meant. It was as if the river suddenly stopped, then turned and began flowing in the opposite direction.

"Jason was right," I told Eden. "He said if I took one right step, the next would become clear."

"Jason?" Eden asked. "Jason never-grow-up Johnson said that?"

"He did," I confirmed.

Eden folded herself into my embrace.

"I kind of miss all that snow," Eden said.

"You do?" I tried not to smile but reached behind to the shadowed side of the rock and grabbed a slushy handful of the stuff.

Eden saw me and snatched it, forming it into a ball. "Perfect snow." She looked at me slyly.

"Oh, no!" I scrambled to my feet.

But before I could get away, Eden pulled out the neck of my T-shirt and dropped the snowball in.

I pulled the shirt away from my stomach, yelling at the cold shock. I turned to throw the snow back at her. Eden went laughing down the trail, collecting more slush balls as she went. I followed, stopping only every now and then to duck.